A Loveliness of Ladybugs

A Joy Forest Cozy Mystery

Blythe Ayne

A Loveliness of Ladybugs

A Joy Forest Cozy Mystery

Blythe Ayne

A Loveliness of Ladybugs
Blythe Ayne

Emerson & Tilman, Publishers
129 Pendleton Way #55
Washougal, WA 98671

www.BlytheAyne.com
Blythe@BlytheAyne.com

A Loveliness of Ladybugs
ebook ISBN: 978-1-947151-95-6
Paperback ISBN: 978-1-947151-92-5
Large Print ISBN: 978-1-957272-05-4
Hardbound ISBN: 978-1-957272-06-1
Audio ISBN: 978-1-957272-07-8

[**FICTION** / Mystery & Detective / Cozy / General
FICTION / Mystery & Detective / Women Sleuths
FICTION / Mystery & Detective / Cozy / Cats & Dogs]

BIC: FM

DEDICATION:

To All Who Enjoy a Good Mystery
With a Few Great Dogs

Table of Contents

Chapter 1
June 1, 2032

"D etective Travis Rusch," my computer whispered as a small image of Travis appeared in the holo.

Ignoring it, I continued to hammer away at my work like a fiend, *trying* to meet my deadline.

"Detective Travis Rus...."

"I *heard* you," I muttered.

"No need to get snippy," the computer retorted.

"Come on Joy," Travis nagged. "I've got to talk to you."

"*Shi-i-inty.*" I smacked my forehead with my palm. "Hang on, Travis. Give me a moment." I looked at what I'd just written. Now, just—*where was I?* I'd lost my thread. Or Travis lost my thread.

"Connect," I said, resigned to yet another setback to my current project. The image of Travis started to grow. "Small," I ordered. The image shrank. There's distraction, and there's too much distraction. "I'm on deadline, Travis."

"You're always on deadline. Look, I need your help."

Dang, he's gorgeous! A*hm* ... don't need *that* thought right now. "You need my help? Let-me-think. *Ah ... no.*" I recalled the last time he "needed my help."

"This isn't like that, Joy." He read my mind.

"Of course it isn't. But I can't, Travis. I've got work to do. I'm sure you'll find someone else to ... whatever it is."

"It's about Teaspoon."

That stopped me. Of course it would. "Teaspoon? *The* Teaspoon?"

"Yep. The one and only."

That's when I noticed in the tiny holo that Travis stood in my front yard, standing by my lilac bush.

"You're *here*."

"I am."

"Is it that important, or were you just driving by?"

"It's important. And I was in the neighborhood."

"*Sheesh.*" I disconnected from him. "Mirror." The holo reflected my image. Not a happy picture. I ran my fingers through my hair, pretty much succeeding in making it stand up in slightly different ways than it had been. Sans makeup. Ragged plaid shirt. Ancient sweat pants. Bare feet. Well, you come without an invitation, you get what's here. "Save document and sleep." My words faded to nothing as the holo took a nap.

I went out to the front porch and sat on the top step.

Travis ambled over, taking in my skewed hair and bare feet. "Lookin' great."

"Sarcasm noted. Did you *have* an appointment?"

"Point taken."

"What about Teaspoon?" I demanded, frustrated. *I had work to do.* "This had better be good, Travis. 'Cause if not, this trick will never work again."

"Ariadne is missing."

"*Supplement Village* Ariadne?"

"Is there another?"

"Ahhh, no. Weird. Ariadne is missing. Kind of a relief, yes?" I was a horrible person. A truly horrible person. I didn't mean what I said, of course. But Ariadne Leysi of *Supplement Village* fame would not be missed by me. She created the most obnoxious ads ever imagined, often holding her bitty-little Yorkshire terrier, Teaspoon, hostage, putting the poor dog in the world's goofiest ads, whether she wanted to be or not.

"*Joy!*" Travis shook his head, a small frown passed over his brow.

"I don't mean it."

He sat beside me on the step, pressing a button on his wrist comp. I glanced at the street and watched as the police department's pride, a spanking new Space XXX Roadster, sighed to the ground.

"Whoa! Must be important for you to stop the steed."

"A person is missing. That's always important. Look, I need you to do—whatever it is that you do to get to the bottom of things—your particular brand of …."

"Insight."

"Right. *Insight*. Woo-woo. Second sight. Mystical, magical insight, to see if we can't find her pretty darn fast before the media gets ahold of this. You know how that impinges on my work environment."

"And yet," I noted, "here you are, impinging on *my* work environment, without even a hint of apology." I stretched my toes out into the sunlight, just starting to peek around the clouds. It would be a sunny day.

"Well, sorry. Sort of. But still, a person is missing."

"A high-profile person who, if not found like, right now, will make your life miserable."

"Yeah."

"So, what about Teaspoon?" I asked. "I still don't want to help you look for this woman, who you'll probably discover on a weekend whirl with one of her gorgeous boys."

"There's a reward."

"I don't care about that! Anyway, my getting my current project done will make me more 'reward' than the carrot you're offering."

"Two-hundred thousand dollars, with more pending."

"*Wha-a-at?*" I paused. "*Hmmm* … let me see…." I drew a deep breath. "Yep. Smells like … smells like a publicity stunt. I'll believe that 'reward' when I see it."

Travis punched a few buttons on his wrist comp and up popped a document in the holo between us. He flipped it so it faced me, which said, under the blazing official icon of the Clark County Police:

Deposit: Ariadne Leysi case, Retrieval Reward: $200,000

"Wow," I said softly. "*That* looks real. Who's it from?"

"It's real." He shut off the holo. "It's anonymous. But I tracked it to **Supplement Village**. The one on this side of town. I think it must have come from the family."

"Yeah. Okay. Still seems like a setup. A setup for one of her goofy ads, and you're going to be caught in the middle of it, and you're going to look *goofy*!"

"Except—one word. Teaspoon."

"What about Teaspoon?"

"The note about Ariadne's disappearance mentioned more concern for Teaspoon than Ariadne. Anyway, the creature is alone in the house. No one to feed it…."

"No one to feed *her*." I was a stickler for respecting animals and not calling them "it."

Travis grinned his half-crooked grin. "Right. *Her*. Anyway, the animal has been unfed since, well, whenever. And I can't be chasing after a dog. I'm trying to find a person. I thought you…."

"You thought I'd break and enter and rescue the little dog."

"I'm not saying that."

"Of course not." I considered the gated community where everyone knew Ariadne lived. "Craptastic, Travis, I'll have to get through that gate at her ta-ta Mac-mansion community."

His wrist comp started rattling off some code, and he stood, rattling code back as he engaged the roadster. "You'll figure it out." He hurried down the path, and the Space XXX Roadster lifted into the air.

"*Grrr*," I growled. He knew me too well. I could pass on thinking about Ariadne. Not because I'm completely insensitive, but because I knew Travis would find her. Probably. However, I could *not* do anything now but check on Teaspoon, defenseless, starving little creature.

A little dog needed me!

Chapter 2
A Loveliness of Ladybugs

I stepped back into the house and went to my bedroom to change—stopping in the doorway when I saw one of my red shoes in the middle of the floor.

"Robbie! What did you do with my other shoe?"

My robo cat came out from under the bed, shaking his head. "I don't know. Dickens did it."

I gestured to the bed, where Dickens-the-bio-cat slept peacefully. "Dickens is sound asleep. I've only been outside a few minutes." I pointed at Robbie. "You're the guilty party. I need my other shoe. I have to rescue a dog."

"Rescue a dog? Oh, boy! Can I come along?" He stood up on his hind legs, putting his two front paws together, looking at me imploringly. It unnerves me when he stands on his hind legs, and I've told him as much. But when he's really excited, he can't seem to help himself.

"No, you can't come along. Now give me my shoe!"

He stooped over, picked up the shoe between us, and handed it to me.

"You know what I mean! It's an ord…"

"I've got it!" He dove under the bed and scrabbled about. I'd better look under there to see what sort of kingdom he's building, but not right now. He came out with the other, somewhat gnawed on, red shoe.

"*Robbie! Why* did you chew on my beautiful shoe?"

"I apologize, Joy." His furry grey-striped face took on an expression of contrition. "I don't know what came over me. I simply *could not* help myself. I guess it's more feline imbedding from the download. I have to say, Joy, I have no idea why a cat would gnaw on a shoe made of wood fibers and plastics. *Blauggh!* Awful, really!"

"Well then, don't do it again!" I looked at the teeth marks and frowned. It was wearable, and I had to get going.

"I won't. By the way, would you like to know what the wood fibers are?"

"Interesting—but not right now. I must rescue a little dog."

"Little dog to rescue. Brilliant. Wish I could come."

"You'll probably see her soon enough. If I succeed in getting her, I suppose she'll come home with me."

"Even better!" Robbie spun, chasing his tail.

"Don't overdo it."

"Isn't that what dogs do? Chase their tail?"

"I guess. We'll have to wait and see if Teaspoon chases her tail."

"T*easpoon!*" Robbie cried. "*The* Teaspoon?"

"You know who Teaspoon is?"

"Who doesn't?"

"Right, she's on the holo ad nauseam. Okay, sleep Robbie." He immediately sank, curled up on the floor, unconscious and purring. The robot cat provided great company, but I wasn't sure how much of my private life was *not* private with his complicated software, all of which shut down when I commanded him to sleep.

I threw on more appropriate clothes, told my wrist comp to bring the car out front, and grabbed my AR, augmented reality glasses. "Robbie, wake."

"Yeah. Who doesn't know who Teaspoon is?" he said, picking up where he'd left off. "I've seen her on your holo many times!"

"Yes. Too many times, in my opinion."

"You don't like Teaspoon?" Robbie asked in disbelief.

"I love Teaspoon. I hate the ads."

"Oh, well, the ads. I don't quite get them."

"Exactly. Me neither. Okay, guard the castle."

"My pleasure." Robbie yawned.

I had hesitated investing in a robot cat, but I'd needed an excellent surveillance system and not only did Robbie come with cutting-edge surveillance capabilities, but, given how much I had to be gone from home, I thought poor Dickens might like the company, even if a fake cat.

And Dickens did, generally, seem to like Robbie. But what I *didn't* expect was that Robbie was excellent company for *me*, in addition to being a fantastic house guard. And further, an entirely unanticipated side benefit was that he could feed Dickens, giving me even more freedom to pursue—whatever I needed to pursue.

*   *

My retro-fitted, self-driving classic Subaru Forester purred in the driveway as I climbed in the passenger seat. No Space XXX Roadster for me. "**Evergreen Estates**—Ariadne Leysi's home," I muttered.

"Yes, Doctor Forest," the car purred, pulling into the quiet street.

As we sped along, I contemplated the gate we'd soon come to, and how I'd get around it. Or through it. Only ten miles distant, we soon approached the long hillside leading up to The **Evergreen Estates**, at the bottom of which stood a monstrous, black, Gothic-ornate, *ridiculous* gate. How was I to get through *that?*

What luck! A big, black, classic limo came rolling out just as I approached.

I nodded at the driver of the exiting car and sailed through the closing gate with impunity. *Hey!* A little dog needed rescuing, and a security gate would not stop me!

My car drove among the stone facade mansions, finally coming to idle at 44455 Rock Creek Lane, in front of Ariadne's home. Surprising! Not the least bit ostentatious. One level, with the apparently requisite stone exterior. Manicured yard. Tastefully understated.

Although I didn't see one single car on the street, I directed my car to go around the corner and stop, hoping not to attract attention right in front of Ariadne's home.

I got out and walked the long block back to Ariadne's house, still not seeing a single person. Avoiding the front door, I headed down the driveway to the back of the house, where I came to a wide back deck. Spotlessly clean, with a few leaves dancing about among the patio furniture in a light breeze. An inviting two-person glider and several wicker chairs gathered cozily around a stone fire pit.

It all did *not* seem like the Ariadne I thought I knew from her ridiculous holo ads. I shrugged and turned my attention to the job at hand—rescuing Teaspoon.

I pushed on the handle of the sliding deck door, hoping on the off chance to find it unlocked. It wasn't. *That's* when I noticed the ladybugs. All around the frame of the door perambulated ladybugs, hundreds, maybe thousands of ladybugs. Up, across, down, and back again. Big ones, little ones, red and black-spotted ladybugs, orange and black-spotted ladybugs, some ladybugs with no spots at all, bright red and bright orange—*delightful!* I love ladybugs, and I'd never seen so many in one place in my life.

Strange and interesting!

As I contemplated the nearly mystical appearance of so many ladybugs—bringer of good luck and jewels, as they say—I saw a tiny bit of movement through the filmy curtain on the other side of the door.

There stood Teaspoon, watching me, her little body quivering. She didn't even bark, surely terrified of this strange person attempting to break into her ladybug protected home. Focused on getting inside, I looked under the adjacent flowerpots for a key, relieved that it was an old-style door, and not a voice or fingerprint activated lock. I hated to reach along the top of the door frame for fear of disrupting the ladybugs.

So I stepped back, activated my AR glasses, and looked around. That's when I spied the ladybug figurine at the opposite end of the deck, which my AR glasses noted had two components. I picked it up and turned it over, discovering a little door on the bottom. Twisting the handle, the door popped open and out fell a small deck door key. *Yay!*

I returned to the door. "Hi, Teaspoon! I'm coming in, don't be afraid!" I unlocked the door and slowly slid it open. The little dog stepped back, but she didn't run away or even bark. She stood there, quivering slightly, watching me intently.

As I stepped a foot through the doorway, a shrieking alarm went off.

Little Teaspoon screamed and tore into the depths of the house.

Chapter 3
A Teaspoon of Sugar

T ravis's holo appeared before me. "Hey, Joy—good work! That didn't take long."

Yikes! He was scary—I would *not* want to be on the wrong side of the law with this intimidating sight. Travis was bigger than life, while the *Clark County Law Enforcement* emblem glowed overhead.

"Criminitly, Travis, you scared me witless, and poor little Teaspoon has disappeared into the recesses of the house."

"You'll find it ... ah, *her*. I had Ariadne's security alarm sent to me, thinking you might be successful in a B&E. Seeing that she has the most sophisticated alarm system money can buy short of human guards, I didn't want to see you here, getting checked into our luxury accommodations."

"*Jail?!* Well, thanks, I guess. Given that I'm here on your...."

"*Shhh.* Trying to work under cover here. Let's not have that be part of the record just yet."

"All righty then, kindly disarm the house while I go through it to find that little dog...."

"And any possible clues where our missing person is."

"Sure. If clues are to be found. I'll let you know when I have dog in tow so you can reengage the alarm."

Travis nodded and clicked off. *Whoa! Blind!* I couldn't see anything for a full minute while the imprint of the holo faded.

Now, to find that tiny dog!

As I walked through the immaculate kitchen, I noticed teapot, teacup, and other tea paraphernalia set out on the counter, not surprisingly, with an adorable ladybug motif. I came to what I assumed to be the door to the garage and decided that would be as good a place as any to see what I could find—especially a carrier for Teaspoon.

As the lights came on when I stepped into the garage, I first noted the little red Volkswagen, familiar to anyone who lived in the area, with **Supplement Village** emblazoned all over it in garish blue and red. But next to the VW sat a subdued iron grey Space XXX Roadster with tinted windows. No one would know who rode in the vehicle. Hmmm, I guess she valued her privacy more than I thought.

I turned my attention to the task at hand, Teaspoon's carrier. I didn't have to look far. Right behind me I discovered shelves identified as: "Teaspoon's Carriers," "Teaspoon's Clothes—Spring, Summer, Winter, Fall," "Teaspoon's Leashes." On a shelf at eye level, I saw a row of pet carriers that would make *Your Pet's Favorite Store* envious.

I picked up a cute little lavender carrier off the shelf muttering, "This should do."

"I should do what?" The carrier asked.

Sheesh! Did I really want to deal with a babbling dog carrier?

"Are you going to talk a lot?"

"Do you want me to?"

"No."

"Then I shall remain silent except as called upon."

"Excellent."

I stepped back inside the house and crossed a wide stone foyer into the nearest room. Double walnut doors stood slightly ajar as I came into a library filled with real books, most of them hardcover. I've never seen anything quite like it.

I put the carrier down and moved close to the shelves of books to read their spines. Tidy labels discretely placed on the shelves, identified the first subject I came to as "Short Stories." There I read the names of the great classics: Chekov, D. H. Lawrence, F. Scott Fitzgerald, Hemingway, O. Henry, even Willa Cather. And recent greats, *in hardbound books. Remarkable!* Listor, Melloum, S. Day, and many others. She shared my likes!

Hardly anyone I know reads anymore. Everyone has to be *read to*. I don't mind an audio book when I'm tired and use it to put me to sleep, but I still prefer reading. Actual reading. I like to make the images in my mind with my own imagination, my own emphasis.

I felt a definite shift in my prejudices regarding Ariadne Leysi as I passed from the library through another pair of double walnut doors into the next room.

Wow! If I thought the library was impressive, it paled in comparison to this room. A grand piano—a real grand piano, not a baby grand—of rich, dark maple, occupied it. On its music shelf stood *Nocturne in E Flat Major* by Chopin.

What next?!

I raised my glance to the walls and nearly fell over as I took in original or extremely fine reproductions of some of the world's greatest works of art.

I moved to the wall to take it all in. Edwin Austin Abbey, Eugene Boudin, Paul Cézanne, Edgar Degas—in alphabetical order with placards noting artist and title of each. Francis William Edmonds, Edmond Fabre. But then I saw a gap. No "G," a blank space on the wall. The placard said, *"Paul Gauguin, Blue Trees"*.

I contemplated the bare spot. Why would only this image be missing?

There could be a lot of reasons. Theft didn't seem likely, though, with Ariadne's sophisticated security and only one artwork absent. *Ah!* I thought with insight, perhaps she had it on loan to an art gallery or some such.

Satisfied with that notion—for the moment, anyway—I continued my exploration. Stepping out of the music room and down a long hall, I cautiously opened the door to the next room I came to, assuming it to be a bedroom and feeling uncomfortably invasive.

But it appeared to be a guest room, in muted shades of pale and dark green, with a bed that looked as if it had never been slept in and curtains that had never been touched. A dresser, a chest of drawers, a lovely but unremarkable graphic on each wall of seasonal nature. Back into the hall, I continued on.

The next door was slightly ajar. A thin line of sunlight streamed through the crack onto the hall floor. I pushed the door a bit farther open and was surprised to see a poster of Valtar Val, a musician and performance artist. Well, yes, I know who he is, but I wouldn't expect Ariadne to have a foggy notion who he was, let alone have an oversized poster of him on the wall.

I stepped into the fairly neat room. Well, ahem, neater than mine so, say no more. I saw a couple of publications on the bed that appeared to also have to do with music and performance art. *Again!* Actual, physical items. Rare indeed. That's when I noticed that the closet door, half open, revealed a young man's clothing. Tee shirts and jeans climbed up a little hall tree, and several wired-up smart shirts on hangers.

I turned around and noticed on a little table across the room from the bed a holo of a beautiful woman. I moved closer and saw, to my surprise, that it was Ariadne. I'd never imagined she could look like this, quietly glamorous, which she never came near to portraying in her ridiculous ads.

In autumn, she'd put on a gigantic pair of overalls stuffed with straw and a straw hat to look like a scarecrow. In the spring, she'd make herself into a gigantic bunny, with false buck teeth protruding.

So—underneath all that hid this beautiful woman ... all righty then. And, furthermore, Ariadne had a young man living with her.

None. Of. My. Business. Or ... was it?

I went back out into the hall and continued down to the end, where it came to another walnut double door. Now I *definitely* felt cautious, while totally prepared for the door not to open at all.

But the door readily opened. I stepped in—and just about fainted when a young man's voice echoed throughout the room, "*Aunt Ari! Why aren't you answering me? Where are you? I haven't seen you in two days!*

Chapter 4
Dog Food and Other Treats

I scurried around the room, trying to find where the incoming linked in. I finally found it on the far side of the ginormous bed, just as the message clicked off. Was it live? No. I found the date: 8 a.m., May 31. Yesterday morning. My entering the room had triggered the message—so Ariadne had not been in her own bedroom since then, at least.

That's when I remembered my mission. I needed to find Teaspoon. "Tea…" I started to call when a tiny little "*ruff!*" sounded at my feet.

"*You!*" I had the strangest feeling that she'd been at my feet all along. And if that was true, what was wrong with my radar?!?

"Let me look around your mistress' room a bit," I said, taking in the carefully made bed, the closed closet door. Everything tidy-pin-perfect.

Nothing to suggest that she'd been kidnapped or had gone off on an unannounced trip. I clicked my AR glasses to replay the garage. I remember seeing luggage above Teaspoon's carriers. Via the recording, I glanced along the top shelf where stood a neat row of practically every size and kind of luggage. Each space neat and occupied. Not even a missing backpack. Anyway, she wouldn't leave without Teaspoon. Although, if a young man lived in the house, there'd be someone to take care of the furry friend.

Hmmmm … I'd better leave a holo note that Teaspoon was in police custody and receiving good care. I stepped out of the bedroom, closed the door, and made my way back through the house to the library, with Teaspoon trotting along beside me.

I stopped at the art wall and had my AR glasses take a bit of video of the gorgeous art, pausing at the blank space on the wall. In the library, I took a picture of the lovely row of hardbound short story volumes, simply for my own pleasure. It warmed my heart to look at those beautiful spines, and I reflected for a moment on all the worlds of wonder these books contained.

Then I returned my attention to the task at hand. Moving to the little lavender dog carrier, I sat on the floor and opened its door.

As I slowly lowered to the floor, Teaspoon moved away from me, glancing from the carrier to me as if to say, "what do you have in mind?"

"Well, little adorable dog, I have in mind that you come with me for a wee bit until we find your eccentric mistress."

Oops! I immediately regretted saying that out loud, as, almost for sure, Ariadne had auto-record in her house. Damage done—I couldn't un-say it! "Come on little Teaspoon," I reached my arms out to her, "Let's go for a ride."

She sat her tiny self down, just out of reach, as if to say, "You've not convinced me yet."

"I don't want to traumatize you. It'd be much better if you just came to me."

She wasn't budging.

I thought about what worked to get Dickens' attention. "How about … *treats!*" I exclaimed.

Wow! Worked like magic! She ran and jumped right into my arms. I felt like a lout, lying to her like that, while delighted that my ruse worked.

I'd make good on my promise and get her some treats. I didn't want to dig around in Ariadne's home trying to find them, so, next stop, **Supplement Village**. I hugged Teaspoon close, feeling an amazing flow of energy from her tiny little body.

"Here's your cozy carrier," I said softly as I put her in the carrier and closed the door.

"*Ruff!*" Teaspoon looked out at me as I stood and picked up the carrier.

"Yes. You will have treats, my furry little friend." I tapped my wrist com, "bring the car into the driveway of 44455 Rock Creek Lane." Then I moved back through the house to the kitchen. I took a 360° vid of the kitchen, with a closeup of the neatly set out ladybug tea paraphernalia.

"Place holo note on kitchen table with comment: 'Please be advised that the little Yorkshire terrier, Teaspoon, is in police custody, and in good care.'"

I stepped out onto the patio, took one last look around the kitchen, then locked the door. I replaced the key in the ladybug figurine, locked its little door, and put it back on the patio.

Returning to retrieve Teaspoon, I grinned at the adorable ladybugs perambulating around the patio door. That's when I noticed a row of them in a thin, straight line, crossing the patio, off into the neatly trimmed grass. Curious, I followed their path. It continued through the grass and apparently into the neighbor's yard on the other side of a solid six foot tall fence.

Interesting! I'd have to look into this ladybug behavior—but later. At this moment, Teaspoon needed treats! My car purred in the driveway. I secured Teaspoon's carrier in the back seat.

"*Supplement Village*," I ordered as I settled into the front, a destination my car takes me nearly every week—*despite* Ariadne's awful ads, not *because of* them! The worst ads, yes, but the best produce and supplements.

"*Ruff! Ruff!!*" Teaspoon responded to my command. Goodness, if my simply saying "*Supplement Village*," made her bark, what would she do when we got there?

"Stop." I got out and turned her carrier around with the opening facing the door, so she could neither see nor be seen.

We—Teaspoon and I—soon pulled into the parking lot of *Supplement Village*. From the street I could see the towering holo billboard over the store. In case you'd almost forgotten Ariadne's awful ads, here a holo reminder marred the skyline, proving that her terrible ads thrived, alive and well—and unavoidable. Last week sported a huge, poorly rendered bowl of fruit with the comment, "*Orange You Glad You Came to Supplement Village Today?*"

Today a gigantic Teaspoon—also poorly rendered—in the arms of Ariadne, and the comment across the sky, "*Doggone Best Pet Food & Treats!*"

The car parked in my favorite spot and I headed inside, making a beeline for the pet section. Although I needed a slew of supplements for myself, they would have to wait until another day. Right now, my mission consisted of treats for a dog. That's when I realized I'd better not go home without something for the cats, as well.

The wall of pet goodies happened to be across from the employee lunchroom. I noted several employees on their break, and, to my surprise, I got an earful. Surreptitiously, I glanced sideways and saw four women and one young—and movie star gorgeous, I might add—man. Three of the women were tearing Ariadne limb from limb.

And I thought *I* didn't care for her! My feelings about Ariadne Leysi were a pale rehearsal to this venom-flinging. The fourth woman tried in vain to be devil's advocate, not that she seemed to like Ariadne, but she appeared uncomfortable with the degree of venom.

The young man, head down, ate his salad, and said not a word.

"She's such a…." one woman started ranting again after a pause.

"If you can't say something nice, Isabel, then don't say anything at all. Let's change the subject," Nancy finally said in a no-nonsense tone of voice.

"Well, I'm just saying, her disappearance is okay by me. Those embarrassing ads! I love working here, but I don't enjoy people who laugh at me after I tell them where I work. And then, for some reason, they always have to launch into a recitation of the latest Ariadne Ad."

Hearing someone *else* say they didn't care about someone disappearing hit me hard. It sounded horrible. No wonder unflappable Travis reacted when I said essentially same thing mere hours before. I felt ashamed and made a promise to myself to be more compassionate.

"I'd like to hear what Aaron has to say on the subject," one of the other women pointed at the silent young man.

The first woman laughed. "He doesn't have to say anything. He's eye candy."

They burst into giggles, agreeing. "True! Lucky us, to have this gorgeous guy come into our midst," one of the Ariadne-haters affirmed.

"Okay, back to work, slackers," Isabel ordered. The four women stood, cleaned up the table, and returned to the floor.

I had touched my AR glasses to record the tail end of the conversation, then I recorded a brief bit of video when I turned my head to nod and smile at them as they came out of the lunchroom.

I don't know how I kept so busy doing nothing, but I think I did a pretty good job of it. Continuing to fain an unnatural fascination with pet goodies, I noted the young man shaking his head as he continued to eat his salad. I thought he hadn't really been paying attention to them, but I was wrong. A strong emotion radiated off him practically out to the walls of the room. Was he distressed over their venom, or in agreement with their outburst? I couldn't get a read on his energy.

Glancing down, my attention was taken by a sign saying the fifty-pound bag of Dickens' particular—very expensive—cat food, now on sale at half price! Whoa! Bonus! They kept big bags of product in the back, and I'd have to recruit someone to get it for me. Fine—I had no intention of missing out on this deal!

I picked up a couple packages of kitty treats. Interestingly, Dickens and Robbie both liked the same one: *"Fairly Fantastic Kitty Yummies."* I asked Robbie what was so fantastic about the fairly fantastic treats, and he said he suspected pheromones had been added in the otherwise ordinary treats. One of the pluses of my robot cat is that his body completely burns up anything he eats. No litter box. Although, if he had one, he'd clean it himself.

Now then, for Teaspoon's treats. Before me I saw an entire shelf of *"Teaspoon's Favorite Treats"* in twelve varieties. I grabbed one of each, then realized I needed, too, to get some dog food. Again, I defaulted to the package brandishing Teaspoon's image, titled, "*Teaspoon's Very Favorite Dog Food!*" I grabbed up a small three pound bag and hurried to the checkout counter.

"It's a special day at **Supplement Village**," Isabel said woodenly, reciting the pat phrase required of employees when greeting a customer.

"It truly is!" I agreed. "My kitty's food on sale at half price makes it a special day. Could you please have someone bring me a fifty-pound bag of **Supplement Village Designer Cat Food**?"

"Of course."

Aaron had come out of the lunchroom and was walking by at that moment.

"Hon," Isabel said to him as he passed, "could you grab a fifty-pound bag of **Supplement Village Designer Cat Food** from the back for this lovely customer?"

Aaron nodded and headed toward the back. As he walked away, I still felt a certain disquiet from him. Or did I simply project my own emotion?

"These are dog treats," Isabel noted, bringing me back to the business at hand.

Darn! She knew me too well. I had chatted with her before about my two felines. "Yes. I have a friend who just got a dog," I lied. "So I thought this would be a fun present to give her. Good for the new dog, as well."

"That's true. Best dog treats in town," she recited unconvincingly.

Aaron came out of the back with my cat food on a cart and, wordlessly, we went to my car. I opened the back, and he plopped the bag of food down.

"Is there anything else I can do for you?" he asked.

To my shock, Teaspoon started barking up a storm.

Arron frowned. "*Sounds like Teaspoon!*" he exclaimed.

Chapter 5
Home Again, Home Again

"**A**h—it does, doesn't it?" I quickly covered my surprise. "These little dogs all sound the same, don't they?"

"Maybe … But … *hmmm*…." A perplexed look crossed his features, while Teaspoon continued to make a racket. "Really sounds like Teaspoon," Aaron whispered.

"Maybe he came from the same litter," I chuckled a fake-sounding chuckle. I changed the little dog's gender, hoping to throw Aaron off. "Ahm, thank you." I moved to the passenger door.

He continued to stand in the middle of the parking lot, looking puzzled.

I climbed into the car. "Home," I ordered.

"Human impediment in roadway," the car replied.

"*I know*." I turned to look at the young man. He finally went back to the store, but hesitated at the door as I drove by. I smiled and waved. Happily, Teaspoon finally settled down.

"Call Travis," I said, once out of the parking lot and on the road.

Travis came on audio only. "You have the dog?"

"I have the dog."

"Did you gather any details of interest?"

"Well, yes, I saw several things of interest, although they don't all have anything to do with what you're looking for. Ariadne has a world-class library. A row of hardbound books of short stories by the world's greatest writers. And even more amazing, she has a *real grand piano*, and priceless art on the wall. I took a bit of vid.

"She's a different person from who I thought she was. There are several other points that are more along the line of what you'll want to know. In private, I believe."

"Right. Where are you headed?"

"Home to unload a tiny dog and a fifty-pound bag of cat food."

"See you there." He disconnected before I had a chance to say good-bye.

*   *

When I got home, I decided to put the cat food away before taking Teaspoon into the house. Travis arrived just as I popped the back of the car open, and wonder-of-wonders, he picked up the bag of cat food before I could get my hands on it.

"Where do you want this?"

"In the garage. I'll grab Teaspoon and meet you inside. And … thanks!"

"My only question," he asked, "is, are you sure this is enough food for your felines? One of which is not even real."

"Hey, they had it on sale. *Half price!*" I watched Travis walk down the driveway to the garage. Didn't hurt my eyes one little bit.

"Little doggie, how're you doing?" I cooed as I got Teaspoon out of the back. I went into the house and met Travis at the back door.

Meanwhile, Robbie came zipping out of the bedroom. "Oh, you have her, little Teaspoon! Let me see, let me see!"

"Hang loose, Robbie."

Travis looked down at Robbie. "You are entirely too human for either a robot or a cat, do you know that?"

The fur rose on Robbie's back. "I am appropriately *both* cat and robot, as per Dr. Forest's preference."

Stunned by Robbie's reaction, I admonished Travis, "Oh! Goodness, please don't upset Robbie. He didn't mean to insult you, Robbie. Travis can ride roughshod over the feelings of others, on occasion."

"I can?" Travis gave me a mystified look. "I believe I made a transparent observation."

"Robbie seems to disagree. Apparently it was an insult."

"*Precisely!*" Robbie nodded, swishing his tail, with an accompanying sound, artificially generated and, quite frankly, scary, that I'd never heard.

I'd never seen this emotion from my automaton cat. What was it? *Ohhh! Jealousy*. Robbie had looked forward to meeting Teaspoon. He didn't want Travis here *at all*.

I hated to do this to him, but I had to control the situation. "Robbie, sleep!" He sank to the floor between us.

"I think he's jealous, Travis."

"Weird, Joy. Just plain weird. A jealous robot. He needs his software reconfigured, or you need to return him."

I shook my head vehemently. "Not in the least. I had him programmed to be emotional, and I'll take the bad with the good. He is so companionable—it's been a pleasant surprise." I gestured toward the living room. "Let's get comfortable and let this little dog out."

I put Teaspoon's carrier on one of my two facing sofas, while Travis sat on the other, then I dug out the bulging bag of dog and cat treats from my backpack.

"So tell me, Joy...."

"Just a minute, Travis. First things first. I have to give this dog some attention so she feels welcome." I spread out several of the packages of dog treats on the sofa beside me, then opened the door to her little lavender carrier.

Teaspoon looked at me as if to say, "is it all right?"

"Joy...." Travis said.

I ignored him. "Yes, it's all right. Come on!" She stepped cautiously out onto the sofa, then hopped up into my lap.

"*Ohhhh!* You're so sweet!" I held one of the packages of treats up to her. "Here's the goodies I promised!" She sniffed at the bag I held, then seeing the array of treats on the sofa, she hopped off my lap and picked up one of the other bags of treats.

"Is that your favorite? Okay. I hope you like some of the others. I bought one of every kind. You say you like all of them on you ad! Or, anyway, that's how Ariadne interprets your bark."

"*Joy!*"

I looked at Travis. "Yes?"

"Can we...."

"*You* told me to get the dog. Now please wait a couple minutes while I make her feel at home. Squawking at me will not help."

Travis frowned. "I run roughshod over everyone, and I squawk. It's a wonder you talk to me at all."

Too cute to see him vexed! "You're not roughshod and squawking as a rule. But, Travis, with me, animals come first."

"Yes. With you, animals come first."

I opened the bag of treats and poured a few into my hand, which Teaspoon readily gobbled up. "Oh, she's hungry!" I pulled out the bag of dog food from my backpack and poured out a handful.

Teaspoon began to daintily but with enthusiasm chow down. "Now then!…" I looked over at Travis.

"Yes, now then … what did you discover at Ariadne's place?"

I sat back, giving Travis my undivided—or only slightly divided—attention. "I don't know if I'd say 'discovered' exactly, but I came upon a couple of notable points. In that amazing music room with the grand piano, and Chopin's *Nocturne in E Flat Major* open on the piano's music shelf, is a wall of art like you would not believe … Edwin Austin Abbey, Cézanne, Degas … incredible! But look here." I pulled up the vid I took of the wall of art and projected it between us. "Missing is 'Paul Gauguin, Blue Trees.' I don't know if it's relevant, but, you know, it looks rather suspicious, does it not?"

"Hmmmm…." was all Travis had to say.

He can be so frustrating! "*Hmmmm*, yes it looks suspicious, or hmmmm, no, it doesn't look relevant?"

"*You* seem hesitant to name it 'suspicious,'" Travis answered. "What's your reservation?"

"Well, first of all, it's the only piece of art missing. If it was theft, wouldn't that wall be empty of art? Then I thought a more likely explanation might be that Ariadne has loaned it to an art gallery or museum, or even a personal acquaintance."

Travis nodded, but still said nothing.

"Anyway, that's what I thought. I leave the relevance up to you. After all, you're the detective."

"But, Joy, I count on your sixth sense. I take your input seriously."

"*Oh!*" I responded, surprised. "No pressure there! Especially given that, as you know, my 'sixth sense' is not predictable."

"No pressure at all!" Travis grinned his half-crooked grin at me. "What else did you come up with?"

"How about this? There's a young man living there." I scrolled to the image I'd taken of the poster of Valtar Val. "Pretty surprised I was to see this poster in Ariadne's bedroom, until I saw the closet full of a young man's clothes. And, for the sake of curiosity, take a look at this." I projected the holo of the glamour shot of Ariadne I'd discovered in this room.

"Who's that?" Travis frowned.

"It's Ariadne. As we've never seen her."

"She's beautiful!"

"Yeah. She simply could not be more different from the way she presents to the world. Why does she do those awful ads, buck teeth, straw coming out of her head, when she's this gorgeous? Everyone hates those ads."

Travis shook his head. "One: everyone does not hate those ads, and two: those awful ads make millions for the Leysi family."

"Really?! I must be from a different planet." I shook my head, mystified, then continued. "Next, I went into her bedroom. The instant my foot crossed the threshold, I triggered a message. A young man, sounding distressed, said, 'Aunt Ari! Why aren't you answering me? Where are you? I haven't seen you in two days!' The message was dated 8 a.m., May 31. So, Ariadne has not been in her own bedroom since yesterday morning, at least. I'm assuming the message came from the young man whose room I'd just left, her nephew. I could be wrong, but it seems the most reasonable probability."

"Interesting," Travis said, without further comment.

"Oh boy, now we're getting somewhere!" Yes, my tone sounded wry.

"Sarcasm noted. Please continue."

"I took this three-sixty vid of the kitchen," I projected the kitchen holo. "She had a tea set out, as you can see. Clean and unused."

"Ladybugs," Travis noted.

"Yes. Ladybugs. Then …" I thought about showing him the image I took of the ladybugs circumventing the patio door, but I decided to keep it to myself.

"Then?…"

"Then I went to *Supplement Village* to get Teaspoon some dog treats and dog food. The pet section is right across from the employee lunchroom, you know."

"No I didn't know. I've never been there."

"How is that possible?"

"Many things are possible, Joy. My never having been to *Supplement Village* is one of life's lesser mysteries. Please continue, is it relevant that the pet section is across from the employee lunchroom?"

"Only in that I witnessed three of the employees verbally hanging Ariadne in effigy. Shocking! Right there on their employer's turf. I noted four women and one young man. The worst of the lot was an employee named Isabel.

"Another employee, who I've interacted with several times in the past and I find quite likable, with a name tag that reads 'Nancy,' tried to temper the aggressive conversation, while the young man sat eating his salad in complete silence. But he had a strong emotional reaction pouring off of him practically to the walls of the lunchroom. I couldn't get a bead on his emotions. Was he upset with these aggressive women, or did he agree with them, and share their criticism?"

Travis began scrolling through data as I talked. "Is this Isabel?" He projected an image of the very woman who had just checked me out at *Supplement Village*.

"*Oh!* Yes, Travis, that's her. How did you do that?"

"I entered 'Isabel, employee at *Supplement Village*' into the Clark PD data bank. She has a rap sheet a mile long."

"Criminy, Travis. What's she doing working there?"

Teaspoon had finished eating, and looked attentively from one to the other of us as we spoke. *Too cute! Too distracting!*

"**Supplement Village** has a program of hiring people who are making efforts to turn their lives around. The owners mean well, but it can backfire, especially given the new laws in the last five years that virtually prevent an employer from firing anyone. The illegality of discriminating against a criminal that one has hired can, as I say, be frustratingly problematic."

"Well then, never mind Ariadne! As a customer, I find that alarming if, in fact, these people are *not* turning their lives around, but, instead, using the job as a means to augment their criminal life style."

"Let's not jump to conclusions, Joy. Innocent until proven guilty."

"Of course."

"Do you want to continue this conversation over dinner?"

What? Where did that come from? Is Travis asking me out to dinner? We didn't need to go to dinner to have this discussion. We were having this discussion right now. "Ah, ahm, *hmmm*." I was stymied to come up with a slightly more intelligent response.

"Great answer, Joy."

At that precise moment, everything on him that could make a noise or alarm or sound of any sort went off. *Yikes,* I practically jumped out of my skin. He put a hand to his ear implant, then leapt up and through the door. "Gotta go."

Chapter 6
Cats and Dog

I scurried to the door and watched as his beautiful flying wonder car took off straight up into the air. He must be traveling some distance.

I heard sirens all around—something big and dangerous unfolding. Now, anyone might think I'd turn on the news and find out what was happening. But they'd be wrong. I didn't want to have sketchy details of some horrible unfolding event to hang my concern for Travis upon.

I turned from the front door and saw Teaspoon standing on the edge of the sofa, watching me intently. I'd actually forgotten about her for two minutes! "Come on, my friend. Let's meet the resident creatures." I scooped her up and returned to the kitchen, where Robbie slept.

"Robbie, wake up."

He leapt up, looking to where Travis had been when I commanded him to sleep, arching his back, hissing. But when he saw Travis was no longer there, he sank down to the floor. "I do wish you wouldn't do that to me, Joy. It's disorienting, and a bit rude, don't you think?"

"You were acting out, Robbie. And Detective Rusch and I had business to attend to."

"Acting out ..." He made the little rushing water sound he makes when he's scrolling through his info banks in order to learn something new. "*Oh!* Acting out is not good. I apologize, Joy. I am, as you know, programmed to have and express emotions. I felt something new with Detective Rusch here, interloping on our moment.

"But I see I had an inappropriate emotion. What ought I to feel in such a situation?"

"I don't know, Robbie. I guess this is a learning curve for both of us. But it would be better if you didn't feel angry with him. Because, although he's a brave and good man, he can be a bit insensitive at times, and say things I'm sure he doesn't quite mean in the way they sound."

"Oh! People can *seem* one way, but actually *be* different?"

"Indeed, my furry friend. But enough of all that, look who I have here."

"Yes. Teaspoon. I see. But I don't want to 'act out' about seeing her."

"Being happy to meet Teaspoon is not acting out."

Teaspoon, who lay nestled in the crook of my arm, uttered a small "*ruff!*" At the mention of her name. I sat down on the floor next to Robbie.

"Well, then, hello Teaspoon. I'm delighted to meet you!"

Teaspoon looked up at me, not sure, I guess, what to think of Robbie.

"It's okay. He's your protector while you're here with us, aren't you, Robbie?"

"Of course!" He reached his nose out to Teaspoon. She cautiously reached her nose toward Robbie, and they touched. That sealed the deal. Teaspoon jumped from my lap, and the two of them engaged in becoming further acquainted.

Fantastic! I could now return my attention to the question dominating my thoughts. Had Travis asked me to dinner before being so raucously called away? And, if so, what was his intention?

Well, my irritatingly pragmatic self said, he was probably *hungry*. And, although not yet dinner time, he no doubt simply wanted to have a relaxed meal while gathering info.

I decided to leave it at that. Then realizing that I hadn't eaten a thing all day. Goodness! It was almost four o'clock! How did that happen?

I fussed around with making a gigantic salad. "Come on, kids, let's go see Dickens." I took my salad and went into the bedroom, Robbie and Teaspoon happily running alongside me.

Dickens, the gigantic, beautiful black cat, remained curled up on the center of the bed just like I'd left him. I couldn't tell if he'd moved a muscle since I left.

I petted him. "Wake up, lazy cat and meet our little friend."

Dickens sleepily opened his eyes and began purring. I put Teaspoon on the bed, and let the two of them get acquainted while I opened my interrupted project. It would be great if I could salvage a bit of this day and get some work done.

Robbie jumped up on the bed and the three creatures settled into a cozy little nap. "Join us," Robbie suggested.

It looked extremely inviting, but I held out. "Got work to do, Robbie." But I couldn't focus on my work, with my mind taken by the mystery of Teaspoon's missing mistress. I needed to allow my thoughts to ratiocinate freely. I took my salad to the bed and settled among the creatures.

I set my mind to wondering where else could I go to surreptitiously learn more about Ariadne. I pulled up an interview she'd recently had, and lo-and-behold, learned that she attended the *Four-Square* church in town … where I've been wanting to go for ages, but it always slips my mind when Sunday rolls around. I'd heard they have great music, and in my view, there's always room for great music.

As if on cue, Ariadne said in the interview, "I go to church primarily for the music. The pastor is a great teacher, but the music at *Four-Square* is incredible."

Yet again, she and I, the two of us, shared values—it was getting spooky. I would go tomorrow to the 11 a.m. *Four-Square* church service. I drifted off into a dream of singing.

Deep in my sleep, I heard Travis calling to me. "Joy, wake up! *Joy!*"

Chapter 7
Pretty Women, Pastel Dresses

Sleepily, I open my eyes, only to see the room in pitch darkness. It was *midnight!* A little Yorkshire terrier slept soundly on my chest, with one cat curled up against each flank. I hated to disturb them.

"What, Travis?" I whispered. "I'm glad you're still alive with whatever you encountered earlier today, but it's the middle of the night, and I'm in the middle of my bed, among three sleeping creatures."

"Oh, right," Travis said. "I'm sorry, I just got off duty. Didn't even think about the time. But I left your place so abruptly earlier today...."

Oh dear, I thought, please don't bring up the dinner-thing now. I don't have the brain power to engage in that conversation at this moment.

To deflect the topic, I became awake enough to blurt out, "I'm glad you called, though. I did some research on Ariadne and learned she attends the **Four-Square** church here in town. Yet another synchronicity between Ariadne and me. I've been meaning to attend that church for ages because I keep hearing about their fantastic music. So, that's what I'm going to do tomorrow, go to church, in the hopes of discovering anything of relevance about Ariadne."

Teaspoon made a sleepy little bark.

"Ah, I've disturbed the family. Sorry, Joy. That's a great idea about checking out Ariadne's church. We'll connect later."

And, as had become usual of late, he clicked off before I could say good-bye.

"Good-bye and good night!" I said to the night, too tired and too reluctant to disturb everyone to get into night clothes. I pulled the bedding from the side of the bed up over all of us and fell deeply into dreamland.

* *

When I woke in the morning, I tried to recall why I felt so happy—what was I looking forward to? Then I recalled that I intended to go to church. Although I didn't generally think of going to church as "exciting," the idea of listening to music, and maybe even singing!, gave me a little rush of excitement.

As I stirred around on the bed and tossed the blankets back over the edge, all the "kids" woke up.

"That was the loveliest sleep I've ever had!" Robbie said, setting his claws in the well-clawed bedspread, stretching his back.

"I slept soundly, too. Outside of Travis calling, that is."

"Travis called? Curious that I slept through it. Oh, here, I see it in my data base. Would you like me to replay it?"

"No, once was enough."

"*Ruff!*" Teaspoon demanded.

I gave her a hug and set her on the floor. "Robbie, could you feed her? I left her food in the living room. And then take her outside and romp around with her for a while."

"Sure! Come on, Teaspoon," Robbie ran out of the bedroom.

Teaspoon looked up at me. "Is it all right?" her look asked.

"Go on, go outside and play with Robbie."

Robbie started to spin and chase his tail. Teaspoon imitated him, barking up a high-pitched storm.

"Okay, you kids, outside with you." I looked at Dickens, who, until Robbie came into our lives, was only allowed to be an indoor cat. And now, as he'd lived his life in the house, he had little to no interest in going outdoors.

"Do you want to go outside with them?"

Dickens opened one sleepy eye and closed it again, which I took for a clear "don't bother me."

I heard Teaspoon yipping after Robbie as they headed for the back door.

"Stay close to the house, Robbie."

"We will," Robbie called back.

Now then, what to wear to church? *Heavens!* Practically all my clothes were black, and it was June, sunny and warm. Black would not do.

I dove into the depths of my closet where I'd not been in a good long while. Much to my surprise, I had a whole slew of clothes I'd completely forgotten I owned. I even had a few dresses. But I couldn't quite get in the mood to wear a dress. Plus, I'd have to think about shoes and dig around for those as well.

I decided to wear my red shoes that I loved so much, even though damaged thanks to Robbie. I found a pair of off-white pants and a pretty blouse in a brightly colored red and yellow flower pattern.

Goodness, how did I come by this blouse? Although pretty, it wasn't like me. And then I remembered that Aunt Claudia gave it to me several years previous for my birthday or Christmas, I couldn't remember which.

This feminine blouse would do nicely for my initiation to *Four-Square* church. Thank you, Auntie! I got dressed and actually ran a comb through my short black hair, put on a dash of mascara and lipstick.

When I looked in my full-length mirror, I have to say I was surprised—a dramatic transformation for little effort.

The question floated through my mind—what Travis would think if he saw me like this, feminine and, yes, pretty? But I quickly moved away from that thought.

Miraculously, I found a little red purse that matched the shoes close enough. I put essential items from my backpack into the purse. Then I slipped on the red shoes and stepped out the back door to be amused by Robbie and Teaspoon romping about in grass that seriously needed mowing. One might think that, as I have an automatic lawnmower, the least I could do would be to keep my grass mowed. But—one would be wrong. I constantly forget to tell it to mow the grass.

"Okay kids, come inside." Robbie came directly to the back door, but Teaspoon hesitated in the yard, looking up at us as if to say, "I'm not done playing!"

"You can go back out later, but right now you have to come inside."

Teaspoon continued to ignore me. Finally, Robbie went back into the yard and herded her inside.

"Good job, Robbie." I looked at the clock—ten-thirty already! "I have to go, I want to be early. Have fun you two, I'll be back in a couple hours." I stepped out the back door and got in the car. "House: lock back door. Car: *Four-Square* church."

"*Church?*" the car asked in surprise.

"I'll take no comment from you! Just drive."

"*Four-Square* church," the car affirmed.

Such a lovely morning! *Why* did I never go for a Sunday morning drive? Almost no traffic, flowers in bloom, sun shining….

"Well," the me who is always ready to respond to my obvious questions said, "you don't go for Sunday morning drives because you stay up all Saturday night working, that's why."

Too true.

The car soon pulled into an extremely busy parking lot, with hundreds of people coming and going. Then I recalled that there had been a service before the eleven o'clock service, which, from the looks of things, was hugely popular.

After the car pulled into a vacated spot, I took my little red purse and red partially chewed on shoes out of the car and to the church.

"Good Morning!" A jolly man greeted me as I passed through the double doors. "Welcome to *Four-Square*." He handed me a little folded program.

"Thank you," I smiled, feeling sincerely welcomed. After I found an aisle seat in the middle of the sanctuary, I glanced around, amazed to see the one-thousand-plus seats almost all occupied—even after an earlier service!

I studied the little program. True to my hoped-for experience, it promised much music. The title for the pastor's sermon: *"New Ways to Look at Old Beliefs."*

Someone's been reading my mind!, I thought. Since yesterday, I'd been on a roller coaster of re-thinking my notions about Ariadne, and I had definitely been in the throes of "new ways of looking at old beliefs." This should be interesting!

I felt like I blended in nicely in my pretty spring blouse, with the congregation dressed every-which-way, from casual to dressy, and from summery fabrics to yes, even *black*.

Before long, people started to come onto the stage. A pianist, a drummer, a guitarist, a bass guitarist, another keyboard player. I was going to like this music! Soon, the musicians took command of the stage, playing a song that everyone—except me—knew, singing at the top of their voices. The words on a jumbo holo over the congregation let me fake it as I followed along the best I could.

A duet followed the congregational singing, then another two congregational songs. After that, a heart-stirring solo from a tiny woman with a huge voice. And, believe it or not, another couple *"everybody sing!"* numbers.

I could go on like this all day!

But it was not to be. The pastor came on the stage, humbly thanking everyone for their musical talent, on-stage and off. I liked him!

Then he launched into a talk with every other sentence seeming to begin with the phrase, "This is for you, Joy

Forest...." I drank it all in like it was a spigot and I was thirsty.

As we reflected on the pastor's words of wisdom, the music conductor led us in yet more singing! After which, the pastor dismissed the congregation with a blessing and an inspiring crescendo from the band and singers. With smiles on our faces—or surely mine—we filed out. In the huge vestibule, if one could call it that, it was as big as the sanctuary, I encountered a great lot of smiling folks, back patting and hugging one another. It seemed I was the only person who didn't know someone.

Just as I began to feel self-conscious and think perhaps I ought to quietly make my exit, someone said something that caught my attention. I looked sideways at a bevy of four tall, pretty women in flowing pastel dresses.

I stepped closer, wishing everyone else would stop having so much happiness and *be quiet* for a moment so I could hear.

"*What can we do,*" the woman in lavender said urgently under her voice, "*to find Ariadne?*"

Chapter 8
Five Ladybugs

Someone reached out and grabbed my elbow. It was the woman in the pastel yellow dress among the group of four. She pulled me into their midst. "Welcome to *Four-Square*," she said in a honeyed voice. "I'm Elvira, and this is Sophia, Mary, Elgin, and Possum."

That's when I saw the short woman with mousy features, completely overshadowed by her statuesque peers, who all came in near my own five foot eleven inches. I doubted that "Possum" made it to five feet.

"You're new here!" Possum said. "Welcome, welcome! We always try to welcome women we've not seen here before. That's how they captured me!" She giggled.

"It is!" Sophia-in-lavender said, laughing.

I smiled, feeling warm-fuzzies among these gentle women. "I'm Joy. Thank you for making me feel welcome. You're so kind."

"Joy!" Elvira exclaimed. "Perfect. We could all use more joy!"

A round of agreement rose from the group. "More joy, more joy!"

"I'll try to accommodate you!" I laughed. I noticed that the five of them all wore matching ladybug brooches. "Oh! You're all wearing matching ladybugs—how adorable! Is there a significance?"

"There is!" Mary-in-pink said. "Ladybugs are said to be the bringer of good things. And that's our mission—to bring good things, and *joy!* to people."

"We got together," Sophia added, "to bring good things to people through our music. We're a quartet here at *Four-Square*. We call ourselves the '*Ladybirds*.'"

"How charming!" I rhapsodized. "The music warmed my heart! I don't know when I've sung so much. I'm sure my vocal cords appreciate the exercise. But … why didn't you perform today?"

"We're performing week after next," Sophia said. "There's so much musical talent in this church that we only get to perform every few weeks. We hope you'll come!"

"Fantastic, I look forward to it!" I couldn't shake the feeling that there was something more to the ladybug scatter pins than they let on. But I couldn't figure out how to "broach" the subject. I took in the serendipity as more than mere coincidence.

Yet more relevant was the compelling sentence I'd over-heard from Elvira. I moved forward in hobnailed boots. "So, I must confess, I overheard you mention that Ariadne is missing. Is that Ariadne of *Supplement Village* fame?"

The five of them exchanged intense glances.

"Yes," Sophia finally said. Her voice softened. "It is. But you must not say anything to anyone. She's missing, *but it must not get out!* It could endanger her life."

"But ... how do *you* know she's missing?" I asked in my own subdued whisper. "Do you think she really is ... or might it be a publicity stunt?"

I was met with gasps all around. I'd gracelessly stepped into a cow pie.

"I know she's missing, because my cousin works for the Clark County PD. He called me right when they learned she was missing in the hopes that, since I know her, I might have an idea where she is, if she'd simply gone away for a while."

"Oh," I exclaimed, hoping against all hope that her cousin was *not* the one and only Detective Travis Rusch. "I take it you don't know anything about her disappearance?"

"No. And it's quite alarming. My backyard abuts her backyard, and I know when she's there as she has certain habits. For example, she sits on her patio every evening enjoying a cup of tea. She chats with her little dog, Tea-spoon—do you know Teaspoon?"

I nodded. Yes, I knew Teaspoon, much better than Sophia could imagine.

The image of the ladybugs parading across Ariadne's backyard to the neighboring yard came to mind. I made a mental note to further contemplate *that* coincidence later.

"She chats with Teaspoon, under the beautiful canopy of twinkling lights she has over her patio. Anyway, she's not done that for several days. No chatting with Teaspoon, no twinkling lights in the evening. Then Derrick called...."

"Your cousin?"

"Yes. My cousin. I felt alarmed when he told me that the PD received information she was missing. They're assuming it's from a family member, but it was anonymous. He asked me to keep on the lookout for her. Now I'm concerned about Teaspoon." She glanced around the group.

"I was just about to mention this to all of you," Sophia continued. "I spent yesterday with my daughter and got home late in the evening. I sat outside, enjoying the lovely evening air, and, as I say, noticed that once again, no Ariadne on her patio. I had heard Teaspoon barking the previous two nights, but I didn't hear her last night.

"Although we're neighbors, it's actually rather a production to get to her house. And unless I feel like going for a walk, it's not practical as it's over half a mile. Although concerned not to hear Teaspoon, I didn't feel like going for a walk after hanging out with my daughter all day.

"Then this morning while I had my tea on the patio, I again noticed that I heard nothing from Teaspoon. I began to worry about her. So, on the way to church I stopped at Ariadne's place. I went up to the patio door, hoping to see Teaspoon. I did not.

"I contacted Derrick and told him of my concern. But he reassured me that, in fact, Teaspoon had been retrieved by one of Detective Rusch's contacts, and I needn't worry."

So … I was a "contact" of Travis's, was I? "That's a relief," I said. "But what about Ariadne?"

"Yes!" Mary said, "What about Ariadne?"

"Yes, yes, yes," they all chimed in, whispering, "Where *is* she?"

As compelling as the subject might be, I couldn't help but notice the remarkable musical quality of their voices, even as whispers, together. I definitely must come and hear them sing!

"So, please, Joy," Sophia continued, "please keep this to yourself."

"I shall! But what do you think? I mean, do you have any ideas about what might have happened to her? Maybe someone had enough of her ads and decided to put an end to them."

What is the matter with me? The gasp of dismay over this thought was even greater than their previous gasp.

"Who doesn't like her ads?" Possum protested among murmurs of agreement. "So droll. So hilarious!"

"That's right!" Elgin, the quiet one, finally spoke up. "The ads are the highlight of my evening. They crack me up! A good chuckle always helps me get a great night's sleep."

"Oh!" I said with sudden insight. I'd been looking—or trying *not* to look—at the ads with altogether the wrong attitude. The pastor's sermon found fertile ground with me! New views on old beliefs—that's what this was about. "So, someone who took the ads literally would be…."

"Would be missing the point," Possum said. "That's right. Missing the point. You have to study the ads carefully. Every ad has symbols or metaphors or…."

"Talismans," Elvira added.

"Yes, talisman's." Possum nodded fervently. "*Talismans!*" She added for emphasis.

Boy-oh-boy, I had some thinking to do!

"Ariadne's ads brought us together," Mary said.

"And Ariadne's ads keep us together," Elgin added.

I noticed a strange-looking little man glance over at us at the mention of Ariadne's name. He sidled over to us.

Chapter 9

Odd Little Man

"Hello, Lowell," Sophia said.

All the *Ladybirds* and Possum greeted the odd little man warmly. "Hey, Lowell," Possum piped up, "haven't seen you in a while. What's been happening?"

"Oh, you know the usual stuff. Busy with my latest work, and all, you know, the usual stuff."

"Hmm, umhum," all the women agreed.

"The usual stuff," Possum repeated.

"What's the usual stuff?" I asked, not wise enough, apparently, to pick up on cues and keep my mouth shut.

"Glad you asked!" Lowell turned his full attention to me. He gave me a serious evaluation, and, not to my liking, I noticed he not-so-subtly touched his collar. He'd just snapped a picture of me!

Not cool.

"Glad you asked," he repeated. "I'm an artist. I'm working on a series titled, '*Dante's Blue Hell*.'" He nodded, giving me an expectant look.

"Interesting," I said, trying to pick up on what the *Ladybirds* avoided by not entering into the conversation.

"It is! Most interesting. Don't want to bore you, but a lot is going into it, and, well, it *is* very interesting," Lowell affirmed.

I waited for him to say more, but, again, he looked at me like it was my turn to read from the script. In my own lame way, I played along. "What's your medium?"

"I work in multi-media. Yes, I take advantage of everything around me to produce my one-of-a-kind images. The *Ladybirds*, and Possum here, know all about my work."

Murmurs of agreement came from the group.

Lowell had stepped into our little circle beside Possum, and I noticed an uncanny resemblance between the two of them. They looked, standing side-by-side, rather like the mouse couple on a wedding cake.

"I think you're new here," Lowell said. "I've not been here in a few weeks, so perhaps I've simply missed you."

"You're right, this is my first time attending *Four-Square*. It's been a lovely experience."

"Oh goodness, we're remiss at introductions," Sophia said. "Joy, meet our friend, Lowell. And Lowell, this is our new friend, Joy."

He reached across the circle and shook my hand. "Nice to meet you," he said.

"Yes, nice to meet you as well." Until, I thought, you just, unethically, snapped my image. For what purpose, I didn't care to reflect upon.

"Lowell," Elvira asked, "How's your garden? Last we talked, you'd planned quite a variety of veggies."

"Oh, the garden!" Lowell signed. "I'm afraid I've not had enough time to properly attend to it. Such a pity. The bell peppers have died before they even produced a single little pepper. The tomatoes vines are sprawling all over the ground as I've not had time to get them up on stakes. The root veggies will probably be productive. I had big plans for the garden, but there's always more 'plan' than 'time' it seems."

"Would you like me to come over and spend some time in your garden?" Mary offered. "I'd be happy to, in exchange for a bit of the produce."

"Oh, no Mary, I wouldn't have you do that! It's my own fault for biting off more than I can chew." He chuckled. "Rather a strange metaphor for neglecting one's garden!"

All the *Ladybirds* giggled.

"Very clever!" Elgin said. "But, really, Lowell, I'd be happy to come over with Mary and pull your garden together. One afternoon this next week would be all it needs."

"Let me think about it. I'll give you a call. Gotta sort out my schedule. You lovely ladies have busy lives too! I hate for you to come out of your way just to schlep over to my place and fuss with a neglected garden."

"Goodness!" Mary said. "Hardly any 'schlepping' involved, we're only a couple blocks away."

"Oh!" I commented, surprised. "You and Elgin also live in *Evergreen Estates*?"

"We *all* live in *Evergreen Estates*," Sophia said. "All except Possum."

Possum nodded. "But I'm working on getting there."

"I see."

"Yes," Sophia said. "When the four of us met, Elvira and I happily discovered that we both live in the *Evergreen Estates*. After that, Mary and Elgin, over time, found homes there, and we have our own little sub-community. We're keeping on the lookout for a cozy home for Possum."

"Cozy little home" was not how I thought of any place in the *Evergreen Estates*, and, it seemed, from her appearance, that Possum would not be able to afford living there. Though I could be wrong.

"Right now the best option might be the Whitney's gatehouse. *Evergreen Estate* residents think it's a ridiculous ostentation...."

I chuckled silently to myself, thinking, "pot, meet kettle."

"However," Sophia added, "the gatehouse would make a perfect little efficiency apartment for our Possum. We're trying to get the Whitney's to agree with us."

"They only have a gatehouse because their house was already on the property, years ago when the previous owners sold it off for development to the *Evergreen Estates*."

"Well, The Whitney's house and mine," Lowell said. "Decades ago I bought five acres, and when the developers came to me to try to cajole me to sell my land, well, let's just say I didn't give in until what they offered meant I didn't have to work another day in my life if I didn't care to."

"I see," I said. That would explain his incongruity with the *Ladybirds*, women who obviously had a certain degree of financial security.

"Where do you live?" Lowell asked me.

Had any of the *Ladybirds* or Possum asked where I lived, I would have been perfectly happy telling them my neighborhood. But I did not feel inclined to tell Lowell where I lived. "Oh, I live in town. Nowhere near the *Evergreen Estates*," I laughed, somewhat uncomfortably.

"Nothing wrong with living in town. There are charming mid-twentieth century homes downtown," Mary said.

"Yes, yes," all the *Ladybirds* agreed. "Charming, charming."

"But, still, It'd be lovely to have Joy in the ***Evergreen Estates***," Elvira declared. "Wouldn't it?"

They all agreed, enthusiastically.

"Would you like us to keep on the lookout for a home for you in the ***Evergreen Estates***?" she continued.

Horrors! I thought. Living in the ***Evergreen Estates***? *Nooooooo!* Fortunately, I contained my emotional reaction. "Ah, thank you, no. Although it would be wonderful to have you all for neighbors, I'm quite comfortable in my little bungalow, near my office across the street from the post office. Everything simple and uncomplicated."

"Oh, what a pity," Possum sounded truly disappointed. "I mean, well, what a pity!"

"No," Sophia disagreed. "I can see that Joy has her life well ordered. She needn't uproot her life to be our friend!"

"Of course not," Possum agreed. "Just saying it'd be nice."

Suddenly, an alarm went off on Lowell's person, and, without preamble, he scurried towards the door. "Must dash," he called over his shoulder.

Chapter 10

Matching Yorkshire Terriers

Sophia shook her head. "That's our Lowell! Strange duck that he is."

"Yes," Possum agreed, "that's our Lowell. But we love our strange ducks, don't we? After all, I'm one."

"Oh no! You're our own little Possum. What would we do without you? You brought new energy into our group," Sophia insisted.

"Oh!" Possum said, "you're gonna make me cry!"

"Well, don't cry!" Mary put her arm around Possum's shoulders, stooping to do so. "Instead, let's go to lunch."

"Oh yes, let's do," Possum exclaimed gleefully. "Come along Joy, join us for lunch."

I was tempted. I was *sorely* tempted. But creatures, and projects, and a chat with Travis, and simply time to do some ratiocination with all the incoming information I was awash in, demanded my attention.

"There's nothing I'd love more, truly. But, even though it's Sunday, I have a huge project I'm in the midst of and must get back to. In addition I have creatures that require my attention."

"Oh! Creatures! What sort of creatures?" Mary asked.

"The usual sort. Cats and dogs." Keeping to myself the actual number of each, and a certain one's identity.

"See? She's really one of us!" Elvira said. "Like Ariadne, we all have precious little Yorkshire terriers. Except poor Possum, because her apartment complex won't allow her to have a pet."

"*Really?*" Matching Yorkshire terriers? "Well, they *are* adorable, and so smart!" I said.

"What sort of dogs do you have?"

Hmmmm … I'd painted myself into that corner. "Well, I only have one dog, and ah, as it happens, it's also a Yorkshire terrier."

"*Ohhhhhh!*" The group exclaimed.

"That's amazing," Elgin said. "You really must come to one of our *Yorkshire Moms* parties!"

I chuckled, amused. Then, looking at them, I realized this was a real thing. I had a mental image of such a festivity. "It must be so cute, all those little Yorkshire terriers romping around together."

"*It is, it is!*" they trilled.

"It's a quarterly event," Elvira said. "We *had* thought of having a monthly soirée, but then we decided to make it seasonal and a bit more special."

"We follow Ariadne's cues in her ads," Sophia said. "There's a seasonal theme, and we dress our doggies in costumes according to information we've each picked up in Ariadne's ads."

Mary giggled. "The objective is to incorporate the cues into our terriers' costumes. Whoever figures out the most cues wins the prize we've all chipped in to buy."

"Yes," Sophia said, "and Mary's grinning over there, because she won the last three prizes."

"She always sees something we all miss," Elgin added.

"I'm terrible!" Mary said sheepishly. "I'm not going to compete next time."

"Oh, no! You must!" Sophia protested. "You're keeping us on our toes. We'll get lazy if we stop trying to get the better of you!"

"It sounds like a lot of fun," I smiled at the enchanting group. "Does Ariadne come to your *Yorkshire Moms* parties?"

"She has," Elgin gushed. "She came to the first one. She always promises she's going to come to the next one, but she's so busy. She does a lot of volunteer work. I do too, and

I see her on occasion but she does considerably more than I do. I honestly don't know where she finds the time."

"Every time you turn around, she's found a new cause to volunteer for." Elgin looked over her shoulder at the thinning crowd. "Looks like they're about to close up the church. Are you sure you won't join us for lunch, Joy?"

Again, temptation struck, but I stayed strong to my commitments. "I would really love to. But, as I say, I have too much calling to me that I can't escape." We began to meander to the front door. "But I look forward to it in the near future, if you'll have me."

"Oh, we'll have you," Possum vouched. "You're one of us, now!"

We went through the door, I to my car in one direction, and they to their cars in another, which were parked near one another.

I paused before getting into my car to glance over at them. Sophia had—and I wasn't surprised—a Space XXX Roadster, a clone of Ariadne's. The other three *Ladybirds* had similar vehicles, upscale but earthbound. I felt a bit chagrined to see Possum climb into a retro-fitted, self-driving Subaru Forester.

I climbed into mine. "Home," I ordered.

*   *

As the car pulled into the driveway, I saw, in my living room front window, three furry heads, watching for me. I laughed out loud. *And Dickens!* Lazy Dickens, right there with the other two.

When I came in the back door, the three of them leapt off the sofa and bounded across the house to me, meowing and barking. Still laughing, I sat down on the floor to play with them. So lovely to come home to!

"Joy!" A holo of Travis came on in front of me.

"Hey, Travis."

"What? Are you on the floor?"

"Well, yes, I am."

"Are you all right?"

I turned the holo to the three little friends in my lap. "I'm super-fine! Nothing like a bit of furry love to make a person happy. Okay, kids, I have to talk with Travis." I stood and sat at the table.

"Did you go to church, like you said you would?"

"I did." I thought about making some tea.

"And?"

The tea could wait. "The music was amazing! I sang my lungs out—super-inspiring. But Travis, the most amazing thing happened. As I left the sanctuary, I heard someone say, 'Ariadne,' and I encountered these four, tall, pretty women, who, it turns out, are a quartet in the church."

"That's relevant, how?"

"Here's the relevant part … they are huge fans of Ariadne's and her ads … apparently there's coded messages in them, or some such. They all live in the *Evergreen Estates*, and one of them is even Ariadne's backyard neighbor." Once again I opted to keep the mounting details around ladybugs to myself.

"That's fantastic, Joy."

"What about on your end?"

"Nothing concrete. It's getting pretty darn noisy around here. Not only her disappearance, but, apparently, the reward for finding her has leaked. Nut cases coming out of the woodwork."

"Oh, Travis, that can't be good."

"No. Not good."

"I'll keep trying to be helpful from my end."

"But Joy, have you not had any of your 'insights'?"

I hesitated. The possible "insight," and what Travis meant by "insight" was my unreliable "second sight"—I was having was simply not ready to share. "No, Travis, not yet. I've had a few twinges, but nothing has become clear."

He nodded. "What are your follow-up plans with these four pretty women?"

"I haven't had a chance to think it through. I just walked through the door when you...."

"*Yip-yip-yip-yip-yip!*" Teaspoon screamed.

I leapt up. "*Gotta go!*"

Chapter 11

The Evergreen Estates—Again!

I flew across the house and into the living room to see Robbie trying to move the sofa, amid continuing wails from Teaspoon.

I hurried to look over the back of the sofa, and there saw little Teaspoon wedged between the window sill and the sofa. I reached down, plucked her out and held her close. "Why did you do that? You could have really hurt yourself." I sat on the couch and cuddled her close. She whimpered and quivered in my arms.

"I feel terrible," Robbie said. "Just terrible."

"Why, Robbie?"

"Because I didn't take better care of her." He hung his head—in fact, he hung his entire body. I don't even know how he did it.

"It's all right, Robbie. And Teaspoon is all right. You can't hold on to her every moment. Come up here with us."

He jumped onto the sofa and stood beside me.

Dickens, who had taken up his nap vigil on the opposite sofa, opened one sleepy eye to take in the commotion, and went back to snooze land.

"You're not upset with me?"

"No, Robbie, I'm not." I stroked his furry forehead.

He purred and leaned into my petting. "Well I'm glad, but you sure are hard to figure out."

"No I'm not!" I laughed, knowing Robbie was quite likely correct. But I also had the thought that, as much as we enjoyed Teaspoon, her mistress needed to be found, without delay. She'd been missing how many days now? Three? Four? I wasn't quite sure. But I *was* sure that the clock continued ticking. Each additional day spelled augmenting odds in favor of disaster.

Then I found myself wondering—*sooo* frustrating—wondering why Travis didn't mention going to dinner again.

"What is the matter with you, Joy?" I said out loud.

Robbie stiffened under my petting hand. "Are you talking to yourself?"

"Yes. I do that, you know."

"It's news to me. So...."

"So what?"

"Aren't you going to answer yourself?"

"Well, yes, probably. If you'll quit interrupting me." I frowned, contemplating the two sides of my conundrum—the one that dreaded the notion of Travis asking me out to dinner, and its opposite—disappointment that he didn't.

"Nope!" I jumped up. "I don't have time or energy for that thought!"

I went into the bedroom and put Teaspoon on the bed. "Are you going to be okay there, my friend?"

"*Arf!*" she said.

Robbie jumped up on the bed. "I'll keep her company. You've got work to do."

"I do, that's true. Thanks, Robbie." I fired-up my neural net. It was time to draw a three-dimensional mind-map of everything I'd encountered, everything I'd learned … and everything I found myself intuiting.

I would not leave out the ladybugs.

* *

Two or three hours later I had a beautiful—to my eyes at least—three-dimensional, color-coded, mind map, with trails radiating out from a picture of Ariadne's house that I'd borrowed from the internet, sitting at the center.

The mind map had the following physical components: Ariadne's house, the **Evergreen Estates**, **Supplement Village, Four-Square** church, and I added my house for no particular reason, skewing the map, way down in the lower right-hand corner. I marked these with in green lines.

There were the people: The four *Ladybirds*; Elvira, Sophia, Elgin, and Mary, there was Possum, Lowell, the employees at **Supplement Village**, in particular, Isabel, Nancy, and Aaron—all designated in blue lines. I included the Yorkshire terriers, noted as "Teaspoon and Friends," in a little bunch of pink lines, as I didn't know their names, and I didn't know where they lived, except for Sophia's Yorkie.

In the "To Be Discovered" box down in the lower left corner I included Ariadne's Ads: clues, symbols, metaphors, talismans. I would have to start watching her ads and look for clues and talismans. If it was just a puzzle I could wile away on a Saturday evening, that might be quite entertaining. But given that we needed urgently to find a missing person, all of the fun was taken out of it.

I also put in the "To Be Discovered" box the miscellany about ladybugs. Some intuition banged about in my head regarding the ladybugs, but I just couldn't seem to focus my mind's eye on what was trying to come through.

As I sat there admiring my work, all the lines pulsing in their various colors—very satisfying—I still couldn't sort out what I might do next. I turned to look at Teaspoon and saw that Dickens had wandered in while I slaved away. I smiled at the three of them curled up together on the bed like little nested commas.

Looking at them gave my heart a rush—they were so adorable! Taking my mind off of my beautiful mind map for a few moments, I had an *aha!* I turned back to it, pulled up a map of the **Evergreen Estates**, and placed it behind the mind map. In addition to Ariadne's house, I knew the location of Sophia's house and Lowell's house. I studied the map to consider where the other *Ladybirds* might live, but, again, no hits.

The niggling at my brain continued until I saw Carlton's house. *Oh!* Carlton had not crossed my mind. He'd been my favorite professor in my undergraduate work, and, as we were engaged in the same field, we'd become friends once I got my doctorate. I used to run into him everywhere, but, I just realized, I'd not seen him for maybe a year. Trying to recall where that was, the Oklumin street fair came to mind.

"Connect, Professor Carlton Mayes." It took a disconcertingly long time, but finally the holo of his beautiful, aged, mahogany face appeared before me.

"Joy! What a pleasant surprise. I've not seen you in ages!"

"I know, dear professor. Entirely too long. I just keep thinking I'll bump into you, like in the past. But I haven't!"

"No. I don't go out and about like I used to. Since I retired, I'm content to stay home and do the work I've been wanting to do for ages. It's incredibly satisfying."

I smiled—so lovely to hear his lilting South African accent, still present, although he'd been in the States for half-a-century. "It's so good to see you and to hear your voice!"

"Good to see and hear you too, Joy. But why do I feel like this is not just a social call?"

"You're right. I have a situation that needs some brain-storming, if you could spare a bit of time. I don't want to talk about it via holo. Might I come and chat it over with you, at your convenience?"

This made him laugh out loud, flashing his big, beautiful white teeth. "I think I know how to translate 'at your convenience.' I'm pretty sure it means 'can I come over right now?'"

My turn to laugh. "Still reading me like an open book! But yes, if it's at all convenient, I'd like to come directly."

"Sure. Come on over. Never mind the house, though."

"Oh, goodness. I have no room to critique! I'll be there in a bit after I feed some creatures."

"See you then."

"Oh, Carlton, wait. I need the combination to your gothic gate."

"Ah, yes, of course. Although it's not 'my' gothic gate, ridiculous pretension that it is. The password is '44444.' They upgraded the gate, and now all you have to do is direct your voice at the lock. Don't even get out of the car."

"That'll be fun! See you in a bit." I changed into my usual black, having completely forgotten that I still wore atypical bright colors. Before changing, I took one last glance in the mirror. Yep ... pretty cute.

Enough of that! I backed up the mind map, then scurried around feeding cats and dog.

"I can handle things," Robbie insisted. "you go to your meeting."

"Okay." I started to shift paraphernalia from the red purse back to my backpack, but then decided that was unnecessary, and threw the red purse into my backpack. "Okay," I said again, glancing around the room. Teaspoon stood poised on the edge of the bed looking at me as if she believed she'd be coming with me.

"*Yip!*" she declared.

"Sorry, dear little Teaspoon. You stay here with Robbie and Dickens."

"*Arrrff!*" she protested.

"Try to keep her occupied," I said to Robbie. "I'll be back in a while."

"Yes. I'll know when you're coming."

"Of course. Sometimes I forget how advanced you are." I threw my backpack over my shoulder. "Bye."

"Bye-bye!" Robbie purred.

I went out the back door, into the garage and climbed in the car. "Professor Carlton Mayes," I said.

"Professor Mayes. The *Evergreen Estates*. *Again?* Are you changing your value system? You're going there all the time lately, when you used to talk disparagingly of it," my car queried.

"No, I'm not changing my value system. But what's it to you if I am?"

"Just making conversation." The car pulled out of the drive and onto the road.

"Sorry, I'm preoccupied."

"I'll just drive."

"Good idea."

We—the car and I—soon arrived at at the towering, black gate. "Drive up to the gate."

The car drove up to the gate. I rolled down the window. "Watch this," I said to the car. "Abracadabra, 44444."

The gate swept open, and I sailed through, like anyone who has a right to be here.

"Pretty slick!" the car said.

"Yeah. Pretty slick."

The car drove among the mini-mansions, finally coming to Carlton's rather more modest, mid-twentieth century two-story brick house. Simple, classic.

"Pull in the driveway." I got out, went to the back door and announced myself to the holo.

No response.

I announced myself to the holo, again.

And then I heard a gigantic crash!

Chapter 12

Professor Carlton's Music

"*Coming, Joy, I'm coming!*"

He soon flung the door open. "Sorry, Joy! Hurrying to answer the door, I accidentally knocked over my timpani."

"Your *timpani?*" I asked, astonished. I couldn't argue that it certainly *sounded* like a timpani. Or a dozen timpani. "What are you doing with a timpani?"

"Creating music!"

I raised my eyebrows and looked at him in surprise. "Writing music? I thought you were working on a profusion of papers."

"I did that all my life. I always have a couple in the pipeline but I'm finally getting to write my music, which I've longed to do." He led me down the hall, and I assumed we'd end up in the living room. But, surprise upon surprise, he opened a door that I'd seen but paid no attention to, supposing it to be a hall closet.

But it was not a hall closet! The door opened to a flight of stairs down into the bowels of the earth. "A basement! Wow, Carlton, you didn't tell me you have a basement."

"I don't generally tell anyone."

"You must have almost the only basement in the **Evergreen Estates**."

"Indeed, I have the *only* basement in the **Evergreen Estates**."

We came to the bottom of the stairs, revealing yet more wonders from my professor friend. I saw room as big as the upstairs footprint of the house, filled from end to end with musical instruments from all over the world, in addition to many items I had no idea *what* they were. I assumed they would make a joyful noise.

I turned to Carlton with a look of amazement. "It's a music museum!"

Carlton chuckled, looking it over as if for the first time. "I guess it almost could be. I've collected instruments all my life, you know."

I *did* remember him talking about collecting instruments during a couple of lectures. But this had exceeded the notion of a little hobby.

"And you're writing and producing music now with your ... music museum."

"That's right!"

"That's awesome!"

"Thank you, Joy." He gestured for me to sit on the sofa, and joined me. "Would you care for some tea?"

"I'd love it!"

"Excellent! Tea for two," he ordered. I expected, like in any ordinary household, a dispensary in a near-by wall would soon ding, or a voice would say, "your tea is ready."

But Carlton shocked me yet again, when a full scale robot came down the stairs, carrying a tea tray.

"Carlton! A life-sized, stair-scaling robot! Your retirement must be extremely comfortable!"

"Hardly!" Carlton scoffed. "I invested. Wisely. Now I can have any toy I want."

"Well, that's quite the 'toy,'" I said, admiring the robot's smooth movements as she set the tea tray down and proceeded to pour tea.

"Gretchen, I'd like you to meet my friend, Joy Forest. She was a student of mine, and then we became friends when we worked on a project together after she got her doctorate.

"*Oh! Oh! Oh!*" Gretchen exclaimed loudly, sloshing tea onto the tray, quivering with excitement. "I know all about you! You're my hero! I've read all your books—repeatedly! I even checked out physical books from the library, because I wanted to touch your words. What you've done for humans, *who need some doing for!*"

Carlton and I exchanged matching looks of shock.

"*Gretchen, sleep!*" Carlton ordered.

She immediately became unconscious.

"*Wow!*" I whispered.

"I apologize! I had no idea she had that behavior in her!"

"Don't apologize, Carlton! You don't have anything to apologize for."

He shook his head and moved from the sofa to across the room."I wonder if I ought to clear you from her data banks? I ordered her to have emotions, but this is too much."

Thinking of Robby's highly sensitive emotions, I said, "Oh no! Don't do that! First of all, given how much she knows about me and my work, it might cause a 'hole' in her neural net to remove that information, and what might happen as a result? It could produce a sort of black hole, or possibly cause the surrounding neural net to crash in.

"Or, two, it might make her depressed. You know, I have a robo cat, Robbie. Well, I'm not as clever at names as you. But, anyway, I ordered Robbie with emotions, and sometimes it's a surprise to see his degree of sensitivity. But it has become less problematic as he develops. For one, he's becoming integrated and forming consistency threads, so there are almost no surprises. And two, I'm getting used to it—it's not as disconcerting as it was at first. New robots are more sensitive until they develop their own personalities."

"And three, and this is the most important point, Carlton—*I like it! Love it!* Yes, unvarnished display of ego. My Id is jumping for joy—get it? Jumping for *Joy?*" I pointed to myself, grinning. "Okay, I'll stop being silly. Here's an idea, you might make a quiet suggestion for her to do something when you wake her, to help take her off this track, while letting her have her feelings."

Carlton nodded. "That makes sense. Most fascinating." He took a deep breath. "Gretchen, wake."

Gretchen's robot body sprang alert. "Yes! Humans need you, Joy," she said, picking up where she'd left off, excited, mid-sentence.

"Gretchen," Carlton murmured, "it looks like you spilled a bit of tea."

Gretchen looked at the tea tray. "Oh! How did I do that?" She pulled a vacuum tube from her body and cleaned up the spill, chatting to herself, reprimanding herself for her ineptitude. Then she pulled a heating device from her body and reheated the tea. "So, so, sorry!" She continued to mull aloud, but she became calm.

I winked at Carlton. "Worked like a charm!"

"Indeed! Thank you, Joy. This is something to remember!"

"All righty! Let's get back to your music—tell me more."

"Wanna hear the music instead of me babbling on about it?"

"Of course!"

I settled in, without any idea of what I was about to hear, but wide open to the experience....

Off in the distance, soft thunder rumbled. The music found the melody in the drops of rain falling across the Kalahari. Great clouds rolled in, the music crescendoed. The storm played out in Carlton's basement, while I felt myself in Africa. Just as the picture became the strongest, *all fell silent*.

I couldn't speak. Finally, I glanced up at Carlton. He studied me, just as he always did in class. Somehow, we're related, and it has nothing to do with skin and bone.

"Oh, Carlton—that's—words fail me. *So amazing!*" I sighed.

"Thank you, Joy. You're the only person who's heard my work, who knows it's mine. I've got it under contract all over the place, but it's written and performed by 'anonymous.'"

"Why, Carlton, why?"

"I don't want fame. I mean, I specifically want *not* to be famous. I've seen how it eats an artist's time. I want to be creating, that's what makes me happy. I don't need any more money, and I've the best friends on the planet. Just in case you have a hand mirror nearby, you can check out my last point yourself."

Thinking about my frustrations with my own relentlessly interrupted project, I understood what he meant. I nodded.

"But let's set that aside now and get to the bottom of why you've come to see me," he said.

"Yes. Let's. I want to talk with you about Ariadne's disappearance."

"Oh, no! I saw something about it on the underground. But I confess, I thought it must be a publicity ploy."

"Me, too, initially. Unfortunately, it's not a publicity ploy."

Carlton's brow wrinkled in concern.

"Detective Rusch stopped by to see if I had any second sight hits when he told me about her disappearance, but I didn't. Still haven't, it's most vexing. I went to **Four-Square** church today and happened to meet a quartet at the church, the *Ladybirds*, in the foyer afterwards. What a delight! As it happens, they're so fond of Ariadne, they all have Yorkshire terriers.

"They even have four parties annually. Apparently, dog costume parties with their Yorkies!"

"Yes," Carlton said. "I know. I go to their Yorkie parties."

"Ohh?" Why would he be invited to a Yorkie party?

"But right now, Joy, my biggest concern is Teaspoon...."

"Don't worry, Carlton, I have her. That was the other reason Travis stopped by, to ask me to see if I could look after Teaspoon. He knows my weak spot. She's at my place, being well cared for. Well, pretty well cared for by me, and extremely well cared for by Robbie."

I saw some movement out of the corner of my eye, and when I turned to look, what I saw was the last thing I expected.

Chapter 13
Yorkies Everywhere!

There stood a little Yorkie on the stairs, staring at me.
Really, they're everywhere!

Carlton followed my glance. "That's Muldoon, 'chieftain of the fortress.' Come down here, you little rascal."

The tiny dog flew down the stairs and into his master's arms.

"*Ach!*" I cried. "I don't think I can take another surprise from you today, Carlton. You've exceeded my quota of shock tolerance."

"That's fair," he laughed. "I'm pretty sure I'm out of surprises." He put Muldoon down on the floor, and the little dog ran over to me.

I looked down into his intelligent eyes, reached down and patted him on his head. "You're adorable, Muldoon, do you know that?" I looked up at Carlton, "Is he the leader of the pack of all these Yorkies?"

"Not by a long ways. Alpha dog is Mary's 'Wolf....'"

"Goodness, with a name like that!"

"Yes, with a name like that ... and for a Yorkie, he's pretty tough. Then Elgin and Elvira's two, and like everyone else, I constantly get them mixed around. Their names are Mulder and Scully."

"Mulder and Scully," I chuckled. "Funny."

"Yes, funny. But again, if you're Muldoon, don't turn you back on them!"

"Well, that doesn't sound good!"

"It's not. Next in the pecking order is Sophia's little gold-colored Poofie."

"Poofie! Oh, cute! But that doesn't seem like Sophia, who's all...."

"I know. She seems all business-like. But she's got a soft side. Wait until you see her with Poofie. And next comes tiny little Teaspoon."

"Oh no!" I looked down at the terrier at my feet. "Muldoon, you must stand up for yourself!"

"Ah, he's a lover, not a fighter."

I laughed. "In the end, little dog, that's the best. But still, I think you might get an alliance going with Teaspoon."

"That's a good idea. But let's get back to the much more serious concern. What are you hoping I can provide you that will be helpful in finding Ariadne?"

"I don't know. I wish something—or *anything*—would trigger my second sight. Where does each of the *Ladybirds* live? Let me see the layout of their residences." I pulled up a holo of the **Evergreen Estates**. "Where do

Mary, Elgin, and Elvira live? Sofia told me she shares a backyard fence with Ariadne, so I know where she lives."

Carlton pointed to the section above his home's section. "This is Elgin's home, and this is Elvira's home." They both had pie-shaped properties, nearly side-by-side, with one property in-between them. It looked as though their two properties might touch at the pointy end of the pie.

"My goodness! They have similar names, and they live close together."

"Not only are their first names similar, but their last names are similar as well. Elgin is Elgin Parkwell, and Elvira is Elvira Parkins. They're always getting each other's deliveries, to the extent that they installed a device to send packages to one another."

"Really!" I looked at the map. "How do they do that without interfering with or irritating the neighbor that's between them?"

Carlton pointed at the tip of the two properties. "At the very point of their two properties, they actually meet without the third property. The delivery shoot goes down Elgin's property, then V's and runs back up to Elvira's."

"Clever!" But my mind already spun around on an echo that teased me, just out of conscious range. I couldn't get a solid bead on it. "What about Mary? Where does she live?"

"Mary is over here," Carlton pointed to the bottom of the map, in his same residence section. "Her house is at the opposite end of the section where my house is."

"*And* her home is opposite Ariadne's property, completely across the ***Evergreen Estates***," I observed.

"So it is," Carlton agreed.

I continued to poke around in my mind at how all this information seemed to be trying to come together and produce a cohesive result. "Listen, I know this is a terrible thing to say, but, Carlton, do you think there's any possibility of dark deeds from any of these women regarding Ariadne? Might one of them be jealous, or … or … I don't know … I'm just musing aloud."

Carlton returned to the sofa to sit beside me. "I don't think so." He paused, seeming to give the thought yet more serious consideration. "No, I really don't think so. I've known the four of them for years now, and have never seen anything even faintly resembling craziness to the extent of kidnapping someone, from any of them." He shrugged and appeared to dig deeper into his thoughts.

"However … and I seriously hesitate to say this, but, Possum is a weird little rodent," he muttered, barely above a whisper.

"Ahh, but, uh, Carlton, possums are marsupials."

"Yes. Well, you know what I mean."

"Not really. What *do* you mean? Is there anything to substantiate your comment?"

"No, not really."

"It seems to me she's sort of a mascot. That might be insulting to some people, but I think Possum would love that description."

"You're probably right. Everyone would be heartbroken if she's not as she seems. On the surface, she's sweet, gullible, and just generally likable. I hope to be able to continue to believe that she's like that all the way through. Since I'm instrumental in her getting a little apartment in the *Evergreen Estates* in the Whitney's gatehouse, I'd be beyond disappointed if it turned out I've been wrong about her."

"*Oh!*" I exclaimed. "*You're* instrumental in Possum getting to live in the Whitney's gatehouse? That's fantastic! You make it sound like a done deal."

"It *is* a done deal." Carlton pointed to the top and center of the map, where I saw the Whitney's sprawling mansion and the little gatehouse at the front of their property.

"The *Ladybirds* and Possum shared with me their hopes that the gatehouse would become available as a residence for Possum."

"It wouldn't have happened were it not for my decades-long relationship with the Whitneys, starting from when Robert Whitney was a student of mine, long, long, *long* ago.

"What Possum does not know, and, of course, what you couldn't know because the *Ladybirds* wouldn't have shared this information with Possum there, is that each of us, the four *Ladybirds* and I, have made a contribution toward Possum's rent at the Whitney's gatehouse to make it affordable for her. She won't even know it. She'll just think she has an amazing deal for rent.

"The builders are finishing a beautiful, modernized, fully equipped bathroom and a little kitchenette, even as we speak. Sometime in the next few days, the Whitneys will let her know they've accepted her application to live in their gatehouse."

"She'll be beside herself with delight!" I grinned. I don't know why it made me so happy, but it did. "Going from living outside the ***Evergreen Estates***, to being inside, at the center of it all."

"That's right." Carlton agreed. "Is there anything else you'd like to know about the *Ladybirds* that I can perhaps help you with? No promises, though."

"I'm all out of questions for the moment. I need to contemplate the numerous *aha's!* I've had. In the meantime, I'd love to hear more of your inspiring music!"

Carlton moved back to the timpani. "If it's music you want, it's music you shall have, my dear student!" He started several tracks, then added live timpani. I started to dance and Gretchen and Muldoon joined me. We whooped, and hollered, and those of us who could, barked....

That is, until a pounding on the door overhead accompanied by the roar, "*Clark County Police!*" stopped us in our tracks.

Chapter 14

In Trouble with the Police

Carlton shut off the music and we exchanged a look. "We're in trouble now!" I whispered.

Muldoon scurried behind Carlton's feet, whimpering.

"It sounds like Travis," I said as we started to climb the stairs, Muldoon and Gretchen following behind.

Sure enough, when we opened the front door, there stood Travis with a couple of officers behind him, the Clark County holo hovering above them. *Impressive!*

"You!" Travis said, as I came up behind Carlton.

"In the flesh!"

"Why am I not surprised?" He looked at Carlton. "What's with all the racket? You've disrupted your peaceful neighbors."

"I'm sorry, Detective Rusch," Carlton answered in his soft, modulated voice. "The devil made me do it." He pointed at me.

"I beg your pardon!" I feigned indignation while the accusation, was, of course, completely accurate. "We'll be good!"

Travis shook his head. "As if I'm not busy enough dealing with real crime!" He turned to his backup. "I've got this. Carry on." He waited for the two of them to disperse before turning back to me. "Are you here because...?"

"Yes. I finally recalled that Professor Mayes lives in the **Evergreen Estates**, and decided to come over and see if anything he said would help poke at my intuition."

"And the noise disturbance contributed to your mental machinations, did it?" Travis asked at the height of his acerbic talent.

"Not directly, no. But, how could anyone complain about the beautiful music?"

"People love to complain about anything. Sound is first on the list. I still fail to understand what loud music has to do with our missing person."

"It doesn't. Can I tell him, Carlton? It'll reduce Detective Rusch's confusion."

Carlton nodded, begrudgingly.

"Carlton wrote that amazing music. He doesn't want anyone to know it. And now you do, and you'll probably put it in a report, and he will no longer be the anonymous creator of music that you're likely to hear on the airwaves and in stores and the like."

Travis registered surprise. "Really! Music? I thought you were a social science professor."

"I'm a *retired* social science professor. I've spent my entire career collecting instruments from all over the world, loving the sounds, and waiting for the day when I retired and could do as my heart directs, which is to produce music. I don't want fame. I just want to create my music."

I nodded and nodded as he spoke, then looked at Travis. "He just wants to create his music, anonymously. And enjoy it anonymously, and see others enjoying it."

Travis contemplated our plea for a few moments. "All right. I get it, keep the details of the music to myself. Not a big deal. More importantly, did you make headway with our missing person?"

"No overt *aha's* just yet. But I'm piecing together a profusion of details, and I'm hoping they reach a critical mass of insight, soon!"

"That would be good." He turned to leave. "You kids keep it down, all right?"

"Yes, Detective Rusch. Thank you for letting us off with a warning!" I cooed in a honeyed voice.

He made a wry face, then waved at us as the Clark County Police holo blinked off, leaving me blind in the darkness.

Carlton closed the door. We stood in the shadows looking at each other, with Muldoon and Gretchen behind us, all of us standing in a little knot at the door.

I let out a deep, deep sigh, and for some reason, Carlton and I started to giggle, somewhat uncontrollably. Soon

Gretchen joined in, imitating our giggles, while Muldoon leapt about, barking and yipping.

Carlton led us back into the living room and we collapsed on the sofas, until our guffaw-fest wore itself out.

"We're a bunch of sillies!" I observed.

"A bunch of sillies!" Gretchen repeated, sitting by me on the sofa, which sank noticeably under her prodigious weight.

Muldoon jumped up into Carlton's lap. Carlton cuddled him close. "*You* are silly. I'm a serious professor."

"Sure," I laughed. "What do you think your students would say if they witnessed the last few minutes?"

"Ahm … I have no idea. They'd be shocked, I imagine."

"Well, that would just show how much they don't know you like I do."

"My dear Dr. Forest, you are the catalyst for this evening's behavior."

I grinned. "And proud of it!" I looked over at Gretchen, intrigued to watch her robotic gears match my grin. "So nice to meet you, Gretchen."

"Oh, it's beyond nice to meet you, Dr. Forest. An extreme pleasure."

"Maybe I'll bring Robbie, my robo cat, over to meet you some day. Would you enjoy that?"

Her brow wrinkled. "I'm not sure. But if you think I will, I'm willing to give it a try."

"And Muldoon might enjoy him, as well. Robbie is wonderful with bio-animals." I stood. "I'd better shove off.

I need to contemplate all the bits and pieces floating about in this database I call my mind."

Carlton stood, and, holding darling Muldoon in the crook of his arm, gave me a big hug. "Great to see you, Joy. You got me into trouble, now I have a police record, but it was worth it."

"Ah, dear professor, you haven't lived until you have a police record!"

We stole through his home in subdued light, and I slipped out the back door. "Will you invite me over to listen to more of your music? I could listen to it all night right now, but duty calls."

"I'm working on a new suite. I let you know when it's done."

"Wonderful!" I climbed into my car. "Ariadne Leysi's ."

The car pulled out of the drive and headed east. But then I realized I needed a good walk. "Pull over alongside this little park." The car turned and paused, purring. "Engine off."

I got out and took in the starry, starry night, the fingernail moon overhead, the wild aroma of magnolia on a soft breeze. What an impeccably beautiful evening! If only I could enjoy it, without all of these rambling, jumbled, demanding-attention thoughts.

"*Ladybug, ladybug, fly away home…*" I recited softly, as I walked along the quiet street toward Ariadne's home.

What were the ladybugs trying to tell me? And w*hy* couldn't I get my mind wrapped around it?

I'd walked about a block when I noticed someone in front of me, walking at nearly my same studious pace. I stepped up my pace, daring to approach him rather than leave him to his peace.

What compelled me? I must be nuts! Someone in the neighborhood was kidnapping people, and I'm approaching a stranger, alone, in the night.

Chapter 15

Incognito

As I came near the man, I heard him humming a tune. It was familiar, but I couldn't name it.

"Good evening," I whispered as I began to pass him.

"*Yikes!*" he cried, stopping short.

"*Sorry!* Sorry! Didn't mean to startle you!" Then I recognized him "*Oh!* You're Aaron! From ***Supplement Village!***"

"Yes. Do I know you?" He backed away from me a couple of steps. Who could blame him?

"No. But I know *you*. You carried my cat food to the car."

He looked closely at me in the evening darkness. "Yes. You had the Yorkie that sounds like Teaspoon."

"Yes. Ah, again, sorry to startle you. So, do you live here in the ***Evergreen Estates***?"

"Yes, I do. Do you?"

"Well, no. I've just been visiting my friend, Professor Carlton Mayes. Perhaps you know him."

"I met him once. But I can't say that I know him."

I nodded. "It's such an incredibly beautiful evening, I decided to go for a little walk after my visit with him. Again, I'm so sorry to bother you. I heard you humming a song I was trying to place. I know it, but can't put my finger on it."

"It's a song by Valtar Val. It's likely you don't know him, but I love his music."

"I know him, and I know some of his music." I put two and two together. "So ... is it possible that you're Ariadne Leysi's nephew?"

He stepped back another step away from me. He seemed about to bolt. "How ... why would you ask that?"

Hmmmm ... more painting of myself into a corner. I couldn't very well tell him, "well, I broke and entered into your home, prowled through it from end to end, went into your bedroom, saw your poster of Valtar Val, and stole away your aunt's precious Yorkie." So instead I said, "Intuition."

"Odd."

"But am I right?"

He moved forward on his walk. "I ... I think I need to be going now."

A desperate situation requires desperate measures. So I said, "I've been retained by the Clark County PD to investigate your aunt's disappearance. That is, if I'm right about who you are. But more than that I cannot say until you corroborate or refute my question."

Then he turned to look at me. I felt an intense stare, even in the dark.

"Yes, I'm Ariadne's nephew."

"Do you know where she is?"

"I do not." His voice quivered with emotion.

"How long has she been missing?"

"Since some time Wednesday. I went to work Wednesday morning, and when I came home, her breakfast tea set sat on the counter. Quite strange, for sure. I've tried repeatedly to reach her, but she doesn't respond. I've been, well, I don't even know what I've been. It's horrible. Where is she? I can't think. I can't sleep. I ... I ... but, wait, who are you?"

I extended my hand. "I'm Dr. Joy Forest. I've been 'recruited,' let's say, by Detective Travis Rusch to see what I can come up with to help find her. The PD is trying to keep this from becoming a huge public ... you know."

"Yes. I know. Well, thank you. I've been trying to understand why it seems the police don't care about my aunt."

"They care. They're on it. But it *is* a frustrating mystery." We began walking toward Ariadne's again. "So, you have a good relationship with your aunt?"

"We have a great relationship. I love her to pieces. And more important than that, she loves *me* to pieces. After I get my AA next spring, we're going to go around the world."

"*Wow!* That's exciting!" I was envious. I had a slew of aunts. Not one had ever mentioned a trip around the world. There's a couple who like me to take them around a grocery store on occasion. I'm happy to do it, but around the world seemed somehow just a little bit better.

"Absolutely exciting," Aaron agreed. "I'm so looking forward to it. I don't much care for organized education, I like to learn things on my own. But she insists it's important to do both. So for her, I'm bored to sleep in most of my classes. But between that and my job at *Supplement Village*, I keep busy."

"So … I'm guessing no one knows you're her nephew at *Supplement Village.* I stood outside the door while those employees ranted about her the other day. I was shocked. It's true I don't care for her ads, but that's not a reason to talk about anyone that way! And it seems obvious that, if they knew you're her nephew, they would not have gone on like that."

"You're observant, and completely correct. The family sent me here, incognito, because of this awful, terrible deterioration of the work environment. All of a sudden, this location has not been able to keep employees for longer than a couple weeks.

"Most of my family has too high a profile to be here without being spotted as a family member. But I'm just a quiet kid. Into music and, ah, well, invention."

"Invention! Impressive." I could see Ariadne's house in the next block. "What a lucky aunt!"

"We're both fortunate. She is not a usual person."

I nodded adamantly in the darkness. "I have come to discover her uniqueness over the last couple of days, yes. An amazing human being." I hated to have to ask him the questions that surfaced, but they had to be asked. "So, with all that bad energy in the store, do you suspect anyone of kidnapping Ariadne?"

Aaron signed deeply. "That question goes around and around and *around* in my mind. A couple of those women really seem to hate her for no objective reason. Okay, they don't like her ads. But, really, is that any reason to hate her, or do some terrible deed?"

"No. It's not. But when you're talking about craziness, all logic goes out the window."

"True. But still, I just don't see any of them going that far. They're miserable in their personal lives, so they come to work and release their frustrations about someone else during their break."

"And I'm worried about Teaspoon, too. Okay, someone left a note that she's in good hands, but I miss her, and it just adds to my worries. I'm all alone here. I talk with the family every evening, but I miss Teaspoon. Except, if someone is going to kidnap my aunt, maybe Teaspoon is not safe at home."

And the thought crossed my mind that Aaron may not be safe in the house either! I chose to keep that thought to myself, making a mental note to have Travis put someone on surveillance duty at Ariadne's house, specifically to watch over Aaron.

"I hope it gives you comfort to learn that *I* have Teaspoon. She's safely at my home, at the moment being cared for by my by robo-cat, Robbie, who adored her before even meeting her, as he watches all of Ariadne's ads, and loves the ones featuring Teaspoon."

Aaron turned and gripped my hand. "*Ohhhh!* Thank you! Thank you! What a relief. I know she's all right with you. *What a relief!*"

"Oh dear, I'm sorry that has caused you so much anxiety." A light bulb went on. "Say! Would you like to stay at my place? It's modest, but I have a guest room."

He thought about it for a moment, but then shook his head. "Thank you, Dr. Forest, that's very kind. But I think I'll stay here, just in case she comes back, or … or anything turns up that.…"

"Right. You're right, of course. Although, I'd rather you be safe. Be sure to keep the doors locked and the alarm on. Let me send you my private link." I sent my personal connect to his wrist comp. "Do not hesitate to contact me and whatever you do, *stay safe!*"

"I will do as you say, Dr. Forest."

"Please call me Joy."

"All right … Joy."

We now stood in front of Ariadne's house. "Is there anything at all that you can tell me that might be helpful, no matter how small?" I asked, hoping he'd come up with something I either didn't know about, or had overlooked.

"Well, there *is* one strange thing. My aunt has a world class art collection. What she has on her art wall is nothing to what's in a vault. She probably ought to have it all in a vault, which I've said to her. But she asked me, 'what's the point of having amazing art if you can't see it?'

"She rotates the art every now and then. But she always changes out the whole wall at once. I'll sit and study the art for hours once I see she's changed it.

"But … this probably seems irrelevant, but right now *Blue Trees* is not there. There's a gaping hole where it belongs. I've never known her to leave an open space on the wall. Maybe she loaned it out to someone. She does that sometimes, but I've only ever known her to loan out art that's not on the wall. She likes things to be just so, and the wall always has a theme. This time it's 'blue.' Most of the art is either titled 'Blue something' or there's significant blue in the image. It's probably nothing...."

"But we don't know for sure, do we? That's exactly the kind of thing I want you to tell me if it comes to mind. Don't hesitate." I patted him on the shoulder. "We'll find her!" I promised, without any clue if my promise would be, or *could* be, fulfilled.

I watched him go inside, and then I moved around to the side of the house where I knew his room to be, and waited until I saw a faint light come on.

I started to call my car to me, but decided I wasn't through walking, and ambled back toward the little park where my car waited patiently.

As I walked, a blinding light suddenly shone down on me from above. I shielded my eyes, looking up....

"*Don't move!*" A tough-sounding woman's voice commanded.

Chapter 16

Robo Cat Makes Supper

"Not moving!" I watched as Travis's Space XXX Roadster floated to the ground. But no Travis.

Well, I guess he has to get some sleep some time. And, it's not exactly "his" Space XXX Roadster.

Officer Jamison recognized it was me she was ordering around. "Oh, hey, Joy. It's you."

"It's me. Walking back to my car, enjoying the beautiful night, and, well, just generally trying to find a missing resident."

"Yes. Detective Rusch gave me a thumbnail sketch of what's going on."

"I intended to tell him to keep a watch on Ariadne's place, to protect her nephew who is living there. But I'll just tell you, as you're here."

"Noted and recorded. I will engage surveillance parameters. There won't be a move at that place I won't know about."

"Good. Of course, you'll let Aaron come and go without feeling paranoid?"

"Aaron—is that the nephew?"

"Yes. He's working incognito at **Supplement Village** as the employee morale is terrible there. I've noticed it myself."

"So have I," Officer Jamison said. "Something just feels sort of off when I go there. Not the warm, nurturing place it used to be."

Wow! She was sensitive. "Something has really gotten out of hand, that's for sure. And our young man is expected by the family to … well, I don't know what they have in mind for him to do. At minimum, report. But now … well, it's too big for him. It's not fair. He's just a kid. We all need to make sure he's safe."

"On my watch, he's safe! Enjoy your walk."

Without further comment, Officer Jamison turned off the Space XXX Roadster's lights and, in stealth mode, whisked up into the sky. Other than it seeming as though a few stars were missing, I could not see even the faintest outline of the vehicle.

I soon came to my car, and with an exhausted sigh, ordered it to take me home.

*   *

Even though it was nearly eleven p.m., three furry little heads peeked from the back of the sofa, waiting for me when I pulled in the drive. Even Dickens was there, in the middle of the night!

They missed me! I loved it that Robbie knew when I was coming home, whether I told him or not. The car parked in the garage, and I stepped into the house. The three little scamps had already rushed to the door.

Teaspoon yipped and barked at the top of her tiny lungs, and Dickens managed to sound a meow or two.

"It's about time, Joy. You've had an unusually long day. An extremely long day! And what have you eaten?" Robbie asked.

I thought for a moment. It seemed that I'd not eaten anything, all day. I didn't even finish the tea Gretchen made for me.

"I'll tell you," Robbie went on. "Your bios inform me that you've eaten nothing. *Nothing!* You're human. You cannot do that."

"Oh, it's okay to fast now and then," I tried to evade the lecture, well earned though it may be.

"Now and then, fine. But you're doing it too much. I made you a little supper."

"You did *what?*"

"I made you a bit of supper. I've watched you do it."

"What did you make me?"

"I did have to get up on the counters to do it. You'll have to be all right, Joy, with my having done that. I washed my paws—all four of them—before jumping up. What I made is simple but good for you. I made you some tomato soup, and a lovely veggie cheese toasted sandwich with, because I know you love them, sweet pickles."

"Incredible, Robbie. *You are amazing!*"

"It's over here on the counter. I couldn't really take it to the table."

I went to the counter and looked at the beautifully arranged soup and sandwich. "My goodness, Robbie! It's wonderful!" I suddenly felt a raging hunger. I didn't usually bother to think much about food, it just took up precious time. But when someone else cooked for me, which never happened, I would usually discover a huge appetite.

I carried the supper over to the dining room table, with my three friends under foot, meowing and barking and chatting. Life was lovely! So sweet to come home to so much love and attention.

I tried to savor the meal, but I couldn't help myself, I wolfed it down in moments. Robbie's read of my bios was right on. I needed nutrition. It had been an unusually long day that taxed my brain. As anyone knows, the brain burns a third of the calories one takes in.

I was depleted!

Robbie jumped up on the chair beside me, watching me eat with a satisfied expression on his striped face. How he communicated his emotions provided a show all of its own.

Soon, I'd inhaled the last crumb of bread. "Thank you Robbie—that was the best soup and sandwich I've ever had in my life!" I declared, overcome now, with a desperate urge to sleep. "What did you put in it? I'm ready to sleep."

"Just nutrition, Joy, simple, good, nutrition. Which you need. You're running around and thinking up a storm and not eating. Of course you need to sleep!" Robbie jumped down from the chair. "Okay everyone, into the bedroom!"

The three creatures scampered into the bedroom while I put the dishes in the Instaclean. I don't even remember stumbling into the bedroom, or crashing onto the bed. I do remember, though, that I had an endless 3-D, cinematic flow of dreams. I knew the answers I was seeking could be found in those dreams. But could I bring them to the surface when I woke up in the morning?

Of course not!

I had fallen into bed with my clothes on, having only kicked off my shoes. But I remembered that superlative supper Robbie made for me. "Oh, Robbie, did I thank you for the wonderful meal you prepared?"

"About ten times, yes, Joy, you have. And, again, you're welcome."

A holo note hung glowing above my neural net. *Urg!* No rest for the wicked! I turned so I could read the note, from my assistant, Wayne, who, given that it was Monday morning, was at the office, trying to salvage the muddled bit of work I'd done on the huge paid-for project with a deadline of this week, as his note reminded me.

"Dr. Forest," Wayne said, "the Gulf States project's deadline is this week. You will not make it. Shall I try to get an extension?"

"Good morning, Wayne. Yes, get an extension if you can. The project went completely down the drain this last weekend."

"I know. Detective Rusch came by this morning to have a face-to-face with me and fill me in. He wanted to meet in person for the sake of keeping it confidential."

"Good! I'll not be able to get my mind to work on the project until this other issue is resolved. There's no point in even trying."

"So I see from the little bit you attempted to do over the weekend. Pretty scattered, if I may say."

"No need to say." Even now, my mind raced with what I must do today. And it didn't include the Gulf States project.

"Thanks for making up a good story on my behalf. Hold the fort. Talk to you later."

"Holding the fort." Wayne signed off.

"Gotta go," I jumped from the bed into the bathroom, taking a dry Instabath and throwing on another black outfit, completely different and exactly the same as the one I took off. Complemented with the same Robo cat chewed red shoes, I threw my backpack over my shoulder and headed for the back door with all three creatures behind me. I stopped at the door and contemplated Teaspoon.

"Would you like to go for a ride, little Teaspoon?"

"You're taking Teaspoon?" Robbie I asked, amazed. "Why would you take her?"

"I'm not sure. It's just … I'm compelled to do so. You know, I have to listen to my intuition."

"But, do you think she'll be safe? You know she's perfectly safe here with me."

"Yes, I know she is." Robbie made me hesitate, and I felt my intuition become muddled. "No, Robbie. She has to come with me today." I grabbed her little lavender carrier, while she barked and yipped in delight at my heels.

"I hope you don't regret it!" Robbie's face expressed more than concern. He looked flat out worried. But I stubbornly moved forward.

I stepped out the back door with Teaspoon at my heels, then situated the little carrier in the backseat of the car. She jumped into the car, up on the seat and into her carrier, quivering with excitement.

Did she know something I didn't? Or did she just hope that I finally would take her to her mistress? I hoped the latter would be true before much longer. If nothing else, I'd assure that she and Aaron would see each other before the day was over.

As the car pulled out of the driveway, I looked at my living room picture window. Only Robbie sat there, Dickens didn't bother to join him. It made me sad, even though Teaspoon was right here with me in the car. There was no getting around how much I already loved that homecoming and departing tableau of three furry heads in the front window.

"I'm assuming the *Evergreen Estates*," the car said.

"You would be assuming correctly." I forgot to ask Carlton if the password for the gate changed on a daily basis, but I guess I'd soon find out. Before long, the giant gate loomed ahead on the road. Like I knew what I was doing and as if I belonged there, I approached the gate and uttered "44444." Presto change-o, the gate creaked open. My car slipped through the opening. "Ariadne's house."

"So I assumed," the car replied.

I had the car park in the driveway, somewhat brazenly, true. But, conversely, I didn't want to leave the car, even more conspicuously, out on the street. I left a holo note on the car's driver's side window for Aaron, should he happen to come home while my car sat there.

I then looked at Teaspoon, and hoped, as Robbie had tried to imply, that I'd not made a huge mistake. I wanted to walk from Sophia's place, by Elgin's and Elvira's homes, and then all the way over to Mary's.

My plan was no more articulate than that. I didn't know what I was looking for, but I hoped it would turn up just the same. I threw a T-shirt laying on the backseat over Teaspoon's carrier. She was practically invisible, and if she stayed quiet, no one would know she was there.

"You stay here, and and stay quiet, Teaspoon, dear. I have to do some reconnoitering, and then I'll come back for you."

She whined a bit, but didn't kick up a big fuss, and I moved out with a sense of purpose, even if I didn't have a clear goal. I walked around the section moving towards Sofia's home. The day spread bright sunshine all about me, with the scent of rain on the air, which I especially loved.

I didn't want to get wet, that's true, but some rain wouldn't hurt. I kept my mind busy with those superfluous thoughts because I just couldn't dig in and manifest productive thoughts.

As I came around the corner of Sophia's section, I saw her on the sidewalk in front of me heading toward me, in one of her signature flowing lavender outfits.

She didn't see me, or anything for that matter, so engrossed in the tiny, gold-colored Yorkie on a lavender leash. I stopped and waited for her to come to where I stood. All the while she had no clue I was there, while she carried on a running dialogue with the tiny dog.

"Little Poofie, my baby, my pretty wittle, puppy doggy. You're so adorable! The most adorable little dog in the universe."

Poofie did not seem to realize, nor to even care that she was the most adorable dog in the universe. She appeared considerably more interested in the bugs on the flowers, and intent upon capturing them. But that didn't stop her mistress from continuing to rattle off numerous praises for the tiny creature.

Carlton had made an understatement when he said Sophia behaved differently when with Poofie. If not for the flowing lavender outfit, I'd doubt who this woman was. Sophia started to walk around me, without so much as a glance in my direction.

"Hello, Sophia," I stepped just slightly into her path. She glanced up.

"Oh! Joy! My goodness, here you are! Have you come to celebrate Possum's move into the Whitney's gatehouse?"

Hmmm, that seemed like an excuse as good as any other. "Is she moving in already?"

"Yes. Right now. The *Ladybirds* are all gathering at the new little apartment. Come along."

"That's lovely! She must be so happy! It certainly came together quickly."

"Yes. When I ... that is, when certain people decide to take action, action takes place! We're gathering Elvira and

Elgin on the way. Hopefully Mary, too, by the time we arrive. Possum will be thrilled to see you!"

Even as she said it, I saw the two matching *Ladybirds* with their matching little Yorkies a couple blocks ahead of us. They waved, but rather than join us, they made a ninety degree left turn. Sophia and I cut diagonally across the street and soon joined Elgin and Elvira, and Scully and Mulder.

I looked around for Mary, but didn't see her. The three little dogs greeted one another, happily barking and behaving as though they hadn't seen each other in a year.

"Joy!" Elvira cried, "what a wonderful surprise! How did you find out that Possum just got her apartment?"

"I didn't. I was going for a walk in the neighborhood when I encountered Sophia and her little dog, who is apparently named Poofie, if her dialogue with the Yorkie is to be taken at face value. I'm here to try and figure out what happened to Ariadne. I hoped a walk around the neighborhood might provide some clues."

"Oh, yes, we are so worried!" Sophia said. "But we must not discuss this right now in Possum's new apartment. Only happy thoughts for her, do we agree?"

"I completely agree!" I said. "It's Possum's day. I'm so fortunate to be here at this auspicious moment, totally by coincidence." The Whitney's mansion loomed up the hill ahead of us.

"Whoa! Kind of ... overwhelming, yes? Out of a vampire movie," I said.

Elgin chuckled, but said nothing. From their silent reaction I felt like I'd—*once again!*—stepped into something I wish I hadn't. I couldn't help it that the mansion completely dominated the horizon! However, as we drew near, the gatehouse became apparent. It didn't have the same horror movie energy as the mansion. The styles were similar, but the gatehouse had a warmth and charm the mansion lacked, looking rather like a cute gingerbread house. I loved it on sight—absolutely perfect for Possum.

I saw Mary, still a block away but heading toward us as fast as her little dog's legs could carry him. Finally, when she saw she would not meet us in a timely fashion, she stooped over and picked up "Wolf," and rushed to us.

"Oh, Joy! How fantastic that you've joined us. Sorry I'm almost late. It seems I can never remember that I'm several blocks further away than you all are from each other."

"You made it in great time," Sophia reassured.

The five of us crossed the street to the gatehouse. As we came to the street level door, we heard something above us that stopped us in our tracks!

Chapter 17

A Room with a View

B *eautiful singing!*
We all exchanged glances.

"Well, I had no idea!" Sophia breathed.

"Me neither, me neither," each of the other *Ladybirds* said.

So! Possum could sing, and sing beautifully!

"Why has she never told us she can sing?" Elgin asked.

"I imagine," I replied, "that she doesn't realize she has a beautiful voice!"

"*Ohhhh!*" all the *Ladybirds* sighed together, making the loveliest musical sound, perfectly accompanying Possum's singing, floating down upon us from above.

But her singing stopped abruptly in mid-phrase. We all stood still, holding our collective breaths.

I reached out and tapped the little knocker in the shape of a hand on the door. We heard Possum rushing down the stairs. Then she flung the door open. "Oh! Everyone! You're all here! Here you are! Guess what? The Whitney's accepted my application!"

"We know," Mary said, giving Possum a hug. "We know!"

"And Joy, you're here too! Oh, how perfect! Come in, come in." She opened the door wide, and we, with accompanying dogs, filed in.

"Follow me up this stairway to heaven." She led us up a flight of stairs, then stepped out upon a landing. The charming apartment opened in a circle around us—the kitchenette to our left, then a little dining area, a living room straight before us, next a tiny bedroom and to our right, a beautiful, sparkling bathroom with a "Health Wall" that had components I didn't even know their function, beyond the usual health bio-meters.

Every inch of the apartment reflected sterile white, which I found a bit off-putting. As if reading my mind, Possum said, "They said I could choose my own colors! Isn't that amazing? I'm going to live with this pure white for a while and see the light and shadows in the apartment before I decide on the colors.

"But the most amazing thing of all is that they are only charging me four hundred dollars a month rent. I've been paying two-thousand a month for a dark hovel that, no matter what I did, I could not get clean. And I couldn't have a pet. Now I can get a Yorkie. I just can't wait. Isn't it exciting? Thank you, Whitneys! Some people are so kind and thoughtful."

I glanced around at the four *Ladybirds*. "Yes, it's true that some people are kind and generous!" I agreed. The Whitney's could readily get four-thousand a month for this adorable apartment. And, thanks to Possum's amazing friends that surrounded me, with the exception of Carlton, they probably *would* see four-grand a month.

Possum led us into the little kitchen. "Look at these perfect little appliances, aren't they cute! I hate to use them!"

"Use them," I insisted. "That's what they're for!"

Possum giggled. "Sure, I'll use them, I'll use them!" Then she took us across to the bathroom. There was room for only one person in the tiny room. We stood outside, peering in.

"Look at this wall of … well, I don't even know what all it is. Health stuff, and … I don't know! I need a user's manual just to be in the bathroom. Does anyone know what this and this is?" She pointed to a couple of the components on the wall.

"I do," Sophia said. "I have the same health wall in my master bathroom. I'll come over some time in the next few days and show you how it all works to keep you healthy."

"Thank you, Sophia, I'd like that." Possum then took us into her tiny bedroom, already furnished with bed and built-in drawers on two of the walls, with a generous walk-in closet, nearly as big as the bedroom.

"Look at all these drawers! I can't even imagine what I'd put in them all! And this closet—I've never had a closet I could walk into! Goodness, I'll have to get some clothes, just so the place doesn't look empty." She took us back across to the dining area. "The dining room is kinda small, but big enough for our group."

"Look, the table can expand," Elvira observed, pointing to a seam in the table. "It's probably voice activated, and can go out into the hall to accommodate a few more people."

"Oh! Do you think so? How can we find out?"

"Dining table, extend," Elvira commanded, and, smooth as silk, the table slid out into the hall adjacent to the kitchen, with plenty of room to move around it.

"Aren't you clever, Elvira!" Possum said. "And how do I make it go back?"

"Table contract." The table slid back to its previous position.

"*I. Just. Love. It!*" Possum sighed. "But here's my favorite space of all." We followed her into the living room. A picture window provided a view of the **Evergreen Estates.** We all crowded up to it, Yorkies leaping about, entangling their leashes.

"Oh, look, Elgin, there's our homes!" Elvira pointed.

"Wow! She can see right into our living rooms!" Elgin said.

Possum giggled, shyly. "I won't do that!"

"Great view of my house as well," Sophia observed. "But you can't really see Mary's place from here." She moved away from the window and sat in a lounge chair with Poofie in her arms.

"Am I relieved, or disappointed?" Mary laughed, as she sat in the chair beside Sophia, picking up Wolf. I moved into the space close to the window that the two of them vacated, while Elgin and Elvira sat on the sofa.

"It's a gorgeous and *stunning* view," Elgin declared.

I remained standing in the window, drinking in the "gorgeous and stunning" view. It was superlative! Far down hill, way beyond the garish Gothic gate, I could see the river flowing. The rich green hillside with towering trees and splashes of colorful flower gardens, and the blue sky enhanced with soaring, mountainous clouds, was as if it came straight from a Maxfield Parrish painting.

I brought my attention back to the near side of the **Evergreen Estates**. In contemplation, I mulled over the much larger concern than if Possum could see inside anyone's living room. I studied Elvira and Elgin's homes with the property between them, thinking about the "delivery system" they'd rigged up that Carlton told me about last evening. Then I looked over at Sophia's home. *Wait!*....

"Possum, dear," Sophia said, "you've been holding out on us. We heard you singing!"

"Oh, no," Possum cried. "Oh dear. I'm sorry! I wouldn't have been singing if I'd known you were right here, below."

"But why are you apologizing?" Mary asked, "Why? You have a beautiful voice!"

"Oh, no. No I don't. You're kind, but no."

"But yes!" Elvira insisted. Scully barked—or was it Mulder?—in adamant agreement.

"Oh, I'm so embarrassed!" Possum cried, stepping into the hall.

Elgin got up and brought her back into the living room. "You must not be embarrassed, dear. We're your friends. Even if you couldn't sing, we'd all be happy to hear you singing, of course! But the point it, *you have a lovely voice!* And we're wondering how we've never known that? How have we not ever heard you in church

when everyone is singing, and we're all standing together?"

"I don't sing. I lip sync, because I want to hear you."

"Well, the cat is out of the bag now," Sophia declared.
"We now know you can sing, and sing you must! Plus you
know all of our songs, do you not? You come to most of
our rehearsals."

"Well, yes, of course I know your songs! You sing the
most beautiful songs. I have them memorized the first
time I hear them!"

"You must sing, you must!" they all agreed, while
happy dogs joined in the confirming chatter.

"Ohh! *Ohhhhhhhh!*" I exclaimed as puzzle pieces
came crashing into place.

"What, Joy?" Sophia asked, jumping up beside me,
peering out the window.

"Oh!" I turned to them, a bit disoriented. "Sorry! Well
… ah, the view, it's just so impressive. It overtook me for
a moment."

"Yes," Elgin agreed. But I could see their confusion
from my outburst. And I felt confused too, a bit. "Sorry
for my somewhat over-expressed emotion!" I turned and
sat on the sofa, smiling, probably oddly, around at the
group. I had to figure out how to gracefully leave, *right
now!*

But there *was* no graceful way to leave right now, so I stood. "I … excuse my somewhat strange behavior, but I must leave. I adore your new home, Possum. It's absolutely perfect for you!" I bolted straight ahead and down the stairs.

I felt them watching me as I all but ran down the hill. But I knew that once I turned the corner to Ariadne's house, they would not be able to see me.

Chapter 18

A Fight for Life!

"Come on, Teaspoon, I need your innate dog-talent." I brought the little dog in her carrier out of the back seat, barking happily.

"I hope you *stay* this happy with me." I let her out of the carrier and clipped her leash to her collar.

"Let's check out the ladybugs."

At the back door I saw the ladybugs still perambulating around the patio door, just as they had been the first time I saw them. And just as they had been the first time, they made their way in a straight line across the patio, out into the grass, and across the yard to the fence that divided Ariadne's property from Sophia's.

I got down on my knees and pointed to the line of ladybugs. "See the ladybugs, Teaspoon? They're trying to tell us something!" And then I had the thought that I must really be nuts. But I was into it now, and I had to pursue my line of thought. I stood, and as we followed the ladybugs across the yard, Teaspoon became more and more agitated, sniffing at the ground and tugging at her leash. When we reached the fence, without hesitation she started to dig frantically at the earth.

"Whoa, wait a minute, Teaspoon. You're tearing everything up." I tried to restrain her by pulling on her leash but she just tugged harder and continued to dig frantically. I finally picked her up and cuddled her, dirty paws and all. She whimpered and struggled to get down.

"We have to go another way, dear little Teaspoon." I left the backyard, walked around my car and out to the sidewalk, taking the shorter distance around the section toward Sophia's house. I passed two houses holding Teaspoon, then I put her down. "Just walk along with me, Teaspoon, okay?"

She strained at the leash, but she had no choice other than to go at my pace. We passed a third house before coming to Lowell's home. I walked up to his front door and rang the bell. Brazenly.

No answer. I rang the bell again. I could hear it echoing in the house. Still no answer. Then I knocked. Finally I heard some stirring inside. A long minute later, the door opened a crack. Lowell stood in the shadows, peering out at me.

"What do you want?"

"Hi Lowell," I faked cheeriness. "I was just visiting the *Ladybirds*, when I recalled your description of your art, and I thought I'd drop by—just on a whim, you know, and see it. If you'd care to share, that is."

Teaspoon at my feet, whimpered.

It was clear that Lowell was torn. Oh, how he wanted to show his work. But he dared not. "Is that Teaspoon? It looks like Teaspoon."

"Why, yes, it is. The *Ladybirds* and I are taking turns looking after her," I lied, "until her mistress returns from whatever spontaneous trip she's decided to take without telling anyone." I chuckled a fake chuckle.

"I thought she had that nephew staying at her place."

"Oh, he's a busy young man. You know how young people are," I grinned and nodded, trying to sidle my way through his front door, thinking how much I wish I could put my AR glasses on. But, of course, I wouldn't dare to make such an unsubtle move—much less subtle than when he snapped a couple pictures of me at church.

"I wouldn't know anything about young people. Don't have any in my life."

"Me neither! But, Lowell, about your art—I thought you'd be delighted to share. I have a small art collection, and I'm always on the lookout for new, promising, as yet undiscovered artists." When I got into lying, I could spin as fast as I could talk. Only when necessary, of course.

Lowell waffled. "Well, I don't have anything completely done yet."

"That's all right. I know how to appreciate works in progress...."

Teaspoon's whimpering augmented, and I hoped I'd not made a mistake bringing her.

"I do have a couple here in the front room." He opened the door just enough for me to slip through. He led me into a dark room—I could make out nothing.

"This one I call '*The Night of Despair*,'" I could barely see him gesturing to something on the wall that was even darker than the room.

"Interesting," I said. "What medium have you worked in for this piece?"

"As I said, I work in mixed media. I use items that are symbolic and meaningful to me."

"I see."

Teaspoon's whimpering continued to augment.

"What's with the dog?"

"I don't know!" I bent over and, against every bit of caution screaming inside me, along with, why-in-God's-name-did-you-not-first-call-Travis?, I unclipped her leash from her collar.

Teaspoon bolted from the room and scampered up a flight of stairs I could barely see in the darkness.

"Where's that damn dog going?" Lowell yelled, running after her, with me fast upon his heels.

I saw Teaspoon take a sharp right at the top of the stairs, Lowell swearing a blue streak right behind her. And me right behind him. I managed to grab his heel, and we came tumbling down the stairs.

Lowell kicked at me. I rolled away from him, and scrambled back onto the stairs, trying to climb them on all fours, with Lowell grabbing at me every inch of the way.

"You're just another witch, another lying witch! You wouldn't know art if it bit you! Get out of my house, or suffer the consequence," he screamed in my ear, now actually on top of me on the stairs.

With every fiber of strength, I raised up and threw him off, managing to gain another couple of stairs before he jumped on me again. The stench of him alone was enough to make me lose consciousness. Had he never bathed in his life?

"Get your stinking body off me!" I cried, gaining another step, even with his weight on me. Only two more steps to go, and then, I hoped, I could send him back down the stairs—before he did the same to me.

I reached the landing, heaving giant breaths, and rolled over, with Lowell under me. He managed to roll over, and now, I was under him.

I saw Teaspoon scrabbling frantically at the bottom of the door, whining and almost barking but so distressed that she could hardly get a bark out.

Lowell jumped up and rushed toward Teaspoon. He raised his foot to kick her.

I leapt up, or more like I *flew*, diving into him, throwing him to the floor. "*You! Will! Not! Kick! A! Dog! You! Bastard!*"

Lowell leapt up and grabbed me by the throat, and we both came to the floor again.

"You think you'll tell me what to do? That dog is as good as dead. But, perhaps you first!" He squeeze the very breath out of me. I brought my knee up into all man's land and let him know who was boss.

Teaspoon screamed bloody murder as she tore at the door. She actually sounded like a small child.

Why did you not call Travis, Why did you not call Travis? my generally soft voice of reason screamed. I reached for my wrist comp on the other side of Lowell, trying to reach around him, even as he strangled me.

"*Nine one one,*" I yelped in the general direction of my wrist, hoping it would register in all this fracas.

Immediately a voice came on "911, what's your emergency?"

I managed to squeak out, "I'm being strangled to death. Contact Detective Travis Rusch, this is Joy Forest."

Chapter 19

Valiant Little Dog

"Connecting with Detective Rusch."

"Joy, where are you?" Travis' wonderful voice came on. "Wait, I have your position. I'm coming!"

I only had to hang on, literally for dear life, for a minute or two—an eternity. I thought I heard some sort of thumping. Or was it the blood in my ears as consciousness began to ebb?

With every scrap of my power, I tried again to throw Lowell off me, truly surprised at his strength. For a wiry, small man, somewhere north of fifty, he was incredibly capable of holding his own. I attempted to repeat my knee exercise, but in my weakening state, I was completely ineffective. I only enraged Lowell yet more. His grip around my throat tightened.

Much to my shock, Teaspoon abandoned the door, turned and leapt upon Lowell, grabbing his ear until he screamed bloody murder. He thrashed about and managed to send Teaspoon flying across the hall. But the distraction let me gasp a life-saving breath.

Looking about desperately for Teaspoon, I saw her leap up, and rush at Lowell again. I heard the blast of a siren overhead. *Travis was here!* Thank all the powers of the universe, Travis was here!

The *Clark County PD* holo appeared above us inside the house. Well! I thought, that's a pretty nifty new asset!

"It's over for you now," I said. "You slimy nutcase!! There had better not be one single disturbed hair on the head of Ariadne Leysi. What is the matter with you? *What is the matter with you?*"

Grabbing onto his bleeding ear, while still trying to lash out at me, he ranted, "That witch! She absolutely refused to display my art on any of her ads! She puts all kinds of things on her ads, but she wouldn't give me a fleeting moment. Here I am her neighbor, and she wouldn't even give me a moment.

"Then when I invited her over to look at my art, she refused to buy any single piece. Not one. She keeps saying she collects the world's greatest art, so what's wrong with her?

"Her '*Wall of Art—Blue Theme*' inspired me to create my new *Blue* series. It will go down in history as the greatest works of art of all time."

I couldn't help but chuckle, even as I gasped for air. "At the risk of having you attempt to kill me again, I cannot help but laugh at your mental derangement. *What delusion!*"

The front door slammed open. Travis flew up the stairs, with Officer Jamison and Officer McGillicuddy fast upon his heels.

Lowell tried to leap up, but Travis threw invisible handcuffs on him before he could make another move. Then he turned to me and grabbed onto me. "Joy, are you all right, *are you all right?*"

"Yes Travis I'm … I'm all right," I took a deep, deep breath, monumentally grateful that I could. I even let myself sink into the muscular security of Travis' chest for a moment, gathering my strength.

I gestured to the closed door. "But I'm pretty damn sure that behind this door we're going to find Ariadne Leysi." I looked around frantically for Teaspoon.

"This madman threw Teaspoon across the hall. Where is she?"

"She's right here, Joy, she's right behind you, watching over you."

"Oh, little dog, *oh, little dog!*" I really could not bring myself to say any more than that. Teaspoon's devotion to me at that moment made me cry. I can be tough in any situation, but that tiny dog's valor was my undoing. "All she wants is her mistress, but here she stands, defending me, all three pounds of her."

Officer McGillicuddy broke down the door, and he and officer Jamison rushed in.

The thumping I thought I'd heard became much, much louder. Officer Jamison came back out of the room. "Detective Rusch, it's a panic room. I have no idea how to open it."

Officer McGillicuddy came back out of the room. "But I imagine this freak show knows how to get into his own panic room. Let's just have him do it right this minute." Officer McGillicuddy frisked him, and found a giant ring of old-fashioned keys.

"This ought to do the trick!" Officer McGillicuddy went back into the room.

I attempted to stand, wobbly on my feet.

"Don't try to stand Joy, you're still weak."

"I want to see. I want to see Ariadne. I want to see Teaspoon reunited with her."

Teaspoon had rushed into the room, leaping about, barking and whining and sort of chattering.

It took forever-and-then-some for Officer McGillicuddy to discover the correct key to the panic room. But finally, one slipped into the lock, and the door opened.

Ariadne came stumbling out, blinking and disoriented, but when she saw Teaspoon, she crumpled to her knees, her arms extended. Teaspoon leapt into her arms. Ariadne folded her to her heart, crying, "oh, Teaspoon, my baby, my little rescuer, my savior. I thought I would never see you again. I truly thought I would never see you again."

She finally raised her glance to all of us, now crowded into the tiny room, mostly taken up with the panic room. "Thank you so much, thank you! I don't know who you are, or how you figured out I was here, but thank you!"

Travis was calling an ambulance to take Ariadne to the hospital.

"Do you need to go too, Joy? I think you should get checked out as well."

"No, no-no-no, I'm okay, I'm fine. I'm more than fine, I'm so happy and relieved."

"Do I know you?" Ariadne asked me.

"No. But, boy! Have I come to know *you* over the last couple of days. You are such an amazing human being. I'm so glad you're ... you're...."

"Yes! Me too, I'm glad I'm still alive too. I have a lot of work to do, and I'm not ready to be done."

I saw her look behind me through the doorway and surmised that Lowell was being taken away. I watched her shudder. I couldn't blame her. What must her last few days have been like? Just the thought made me shudder as well.

"Are you cold, Joy, are you cold?" Travis asked, putting his arm around my shoulders.

"No Travis, I'm not. I just ... for a moment ... thought about what Ariadne's last few days must've been like." I looked at her. "I'm so sorry, so profoundly sorry, that I couldn't figure out where you were a couple days ago. I don't know why it took me so long. All the pieces waited for me to put them together, and somewhere in me I knew the solution. *I knew this.* But I just couldn't bring it to the surface of my mind...."

"*You* found me?"

"All by herself," Travis said. "All by herself, when she should have," he looked at me hard, "when she *should have* called me before coming here all alone."

I nodded in agreement, which hurt from the damage Lowell had done to my throat. "You're absolutely right, Travis. Lying there on the floor thinking that I had just taken my last breath, I berated myself for not having called you. But when I'm in the throes of my second sight, it's not a place where I do the best real-world thinking. What's important right now is that Ariadne has been returned to us, to create yet another series of ads, and to continue to do all the other wonderful work she does for the human family."

"My ads were not on the top of my mind the last few days," Ariadne said. "What *was* on the top of my mind were the programs I've initiated to help people. I found myself hoping and praying that whatever happened to me, my work would continue."

"I believe you can rest assured that your work would be carried on," I said warmly. "From what I learned about you, and what I learned people feel about you, is so touching. Your work will carry-on. But… only *you* can produce your ads. There's not another Ariadne Leysi. The Creator pretty much threw away the mold after manifesting you."

"That's very kind. Not true, of course, but kind."

The door downstairs, standing open, now issued in the paramedics. They came up the stairs with a floating gurney. They lifted Ariadne onto it, with Teaspoon still in her arms.

Chapter 20

Three Days Later

Much had transpired in the previous three days. Ariadne, it happily turned out, had suffered the ordeal and came out in fine condition. I, however sustained a bruised pharynx, a sprained thumb—now wrapped up like a mummy—two, painful but improving cracked ribs, and other body-wide bruises. Not too bad for being strangled and thrown about like a rag doll.

Ariadne invited me over to tea. She wanted to thank me some more—entirely unnecessary!—and she wanted to know more details of all that went on while she was held captive.

So the two of us, with Teaspoon in heaven leaping from Ariadne's lap to mine, which certainly warmed the cockles of my heart the first time she hopped over to me, sat out on her cozy patio, sipping tea from the charming ladybug tea set, while, I noticed, the ladybugs still made their circuit around the door. But they no longer crossed the patio to the back fence.

Ariadne poured me another cup of tea. "So, how *did* you determine I was at Lowell's, dear Joy? I'm confused about that."

"All the clues sat waiting, and, like I said, I don't know why it took me days to see what lay right in front of me. The ladybugs provided the first and biggest clue. The ladybugs are happily at home in your home. But when they crossed your backyard and formed a straight line all the way to the back fence line, that seemed strange. I thought they were going into Sophia's yard and felt certain that their behavior offered relevant information—but what was it?

"I let myself become misdirected by trying to understand how Sophia figured into your disappearance. I couldn't get a read on her that she was anything other than a friend, someone who genuinely likes you, and who had no need to do anything bad to you. She's obviously affluent, and well, like I say, I got caught up in trying to make that make sense."

"In other words, dear Sophia was a suspect?"

"Well, yes, sort of. But only in *my* mind. I didn't express the thought to anyone, not even Detective Rusch, because it just didn't fit.

"Then when I talked with Carlton that lovely evening, and he pointed out where Elgin and Elvira live, and we talked about how their two pie-shaped properties come together at a point, that's when I began to have the distinct feeling that I had missed something. Sophia's property is not pie-shaped, but Lowell's is.

"In Possum's darling new apartment I looked down on Elgin and Elvira's properties, and physically saw how they came together, and then looked over at Sophia's and Lowell's homes ... that's when, with lightning clarity, I saw that the ladybugs shot an arrow to *Lowell's* house, *not Sophia's!*

"Without preamble, I, somewhat embarrassingly, bolted from Possum's place and flew down the hill to get Teaspoon, because I needed her natural dog ability to track and find you. I apologize for endangering her, but I knew that's all she wanted, and your life was in danger. Sometimes one has to prioritize awful choices."

Ariadne nodded. "Sometimes one does." She smiled down at Teaspoon in my lap, who jumped up and hopped back across to Ariadne's lap.

We both giggled.

"She's so grateful that you found me."

"I know. And I loved having her for a couple days. My highly emotional robo cat is distraught that she's gone. Although, at the same time, he's ecstatic that you've been returned to the land of the living. He watches all your ads, and is, of course, especially fond of the ones with Teaspoon. Even more so now. I'll catch him watching old ads featuring Teaspoon."

"Oh, dear, we can't have your robo cat unhappy! You must bring him over for a play date soon."

"Oh, Ariadne, that is so thoughtful. He'd love it!"

"So, it was you who came and got Teaspoon?"

"Yes. Detective Rusch asked me to try to sort out where you were. He wanted to not let it get out that you were missing due to the media circus it would inspire, making it more difficult to find you, along with having to field the questions and deal with the nutcases coming out of the woodwork."

Ariadne nodded. "Indeed. I have to deal with enough nutcases, in the wake of any new ad campaign."

"Really? Goodness, I wonder why you keep making them!"

"Well, dear Joy, not only do they generate a ridiculous amount of money for **Supplement Village**, but, again, and more importantly, it furthers my several causes. More money I don't particularly need, but finding people who share my values and help my causes is something I *do* need. Equally important to me, personally, are the many wonderful people I've met in the process. It's so nurturing to spend time with people from one's own tribe. Like you, Joy."

"Thank you, Ariadne, I agree, completely. So lovely to get to know you. And the *Ladybirds*, who think the world of you."

"Ah! The lovely *Ladybirds*! I wish I could get to church more often to hear them, and all the other wondrous music there, but I do so much traveling."

"Last Sunday was the first time I've gone to **Four-Square** church," I said. "And I was, frankly, stunned by the talent. The *Ladybirds* are performing Sunday after next. I'm so looking forward to it!"

"I'm glad to hear that, because I have a treat for you."

"Oh, really?" I asked.

But Ariadne just smiled a Mona Lisa smile.

"I do have a couple burning questions, if I may...."

"Of course, Joy, ask anything."

"I'm wondering how Lowell managed to kidnap you in the first place ... if it's not too painful to discuss."

"No. In fact, it'll feel good to talk about it to someone other than a shrink, nice shrink that he was. It's not the least bit complicated, and I was an utter fool. I'm so glad I didn't take Teaspoon with me. I almost did, but for some reason I didn't.

"Lowell had been bothering and *bothering* me to come and look at his 'art.' I'd claimed dozens of times that I was too busy, but last Wednesday he just broke me down. He called me before I even had my morning tea, and I had to do some traveling that day. So I just up and walked over to his place.

"He invited me into his home. Even as I stepped across the threshold, I had a creepy feeling. Well first of all…."

"First of all," I interjected, "it's dark, and creepy, and *dreadful*."

"Exactly! Dreadful. But, foolishly, I entered. He took me through his dark house, into his dark workroom and showed me these dark, what he called, 'mixed media works of art.' None of which I could clearly see, and, none of which, I felt certain, I would *want* to clearly see.

"He tried to get me to commit to buying something, anything. Honestly, as I walked over I had the conversation in my mind to buy something of his if I could bring myself to purchase anything, just to get him to leave me alone."

"Well," I suggested, "I imagine that would simply have opened the gates of Lowell hell. He would have dunned you to death to buy more."

"Yes. That thought also crossed my mind. But, in any case, it was irrelevant because there was nothing that I even wanted to have in my hands, let alone in my home.

When I resisted, attempting to be as polite as I possibly could, he became strangely quiet. Relieved, it seemed he was going to let me off without further nagging. Fantastic, I thought.

"Instead, he quietly, and in fact quite civilly, invited me to see some sketches by a couple of emerging artists that he said he had in a safe upstairs.

"I was surprised when he dropped the names of young, and as yet undiscovered, artists I'm familiar with. My extreme interest in seeing any work of theirs might have clouded my rational thinking even more. I'd not realized that he overheard me mention their names at my *Blue Wall Art* party, and made a note of them.

So I trotted right up the stairs behind him and into that horrifying room, where the panic room door stood open. He *planned* to kidnap me if I didn't buy any of his works. It was not spontaneous. He had been thinking about kidnapping me for a good long while.

"And the rest, as they say, is history. One little push, the door slammed, and that was that."

I reached across and grabbed her hands. "Oh, Ariadne! How horrible, *how horrible!* I'm sorry to make you revisit it."

"No, no, Joy. No, truly as I say, it's a relief to just talk about it out loud in my own home with a friend."

My heart stirred by the way she said the word "friend." "It's behind you now, dear Ariadne."

"Yes. Well and truly behind me. But you, Joy, have suffered all these injuries," she gestured from my head to feet, "on my behalf. Saying thank you is too small in the wake of what you've done for me."

"I would do it again! I would do it for anyone! I'm pretty tough. I've taken a slew of self-defense courses and have earned a purple belt in jiu jitsu—although my instructor would have been disappointed in my performance. I was taken by surprise by Lowell's strength! Anyway, I'm on the mend, taking it easy."

"I'm relieved to hear it, Joy. I'm still taking it easy, as well. And now, please tell me your second burning question?"

"My second burning question is how *ever* did Lowell get his hands on your '*Blue Trees*'?"

"Didn't I wonder that myself?! But thanks to Officer Rusch, he solved that mystery. He came over with a request to access the house surveillance system. On it, he showed me Lowell, lurking in the shadows of the back door in the driveway when Aaron stepped out into the yard with Teaspoon Wednesday evening.

"Aaron had the house alarm turned off when he stepped outside. Lowell brazenly slipped in through the patio door, stole straight to the art wall, took *Blue Trees*, and slipped out the front door. He stood right in the front doorway portico and slipped my precious art into a back-pack.

"On the twenty-four hour surveillance system he's barely a shadowy blip. With the house alarm off, and the few seconds it took him to do his dirty deed, it didn't turn up until Officer Rusch figured out what to look for."

"Incredible, brazen nut-case!" I whispered. "I mean Lowell, not Officer Rusch," I added, giggling.

Ariadne chuckled. "Yes, Lowell. Nuts. So, so true. My '*Blue Trees*' is not the original, but it's an extremely fine and expensive rendition. It's always been one of my favorite works of art." Ariadne signed deeply. "You move into a gated community in the hopes of acquiring some measure of security—until you discover that the vermin is locked *inside the walls with you*."

I nodded and shuddered involuntarily.

Right then, Aaron came out onto the patio to join us, grabbing a chair and pulling it close to Ariadne.

"Just get off work?" she asked, smiling warmly at him.

"Yes." He looked down at Teaspoon, who, nearly beside herself, leapt from Ariadne's lap into Aaron's. His somewhat anxious look turned to smiles as he gave Teaspoon a big hug. "Love you too, little friend." He reached over and took hold of Ariadne's hand. "Oh, Auntie … I.…"

"I know, dear. It was so difficult, but I'm all right. Please stop worrying."

"Well, I feel unbearably guilty." He looked at me, gratitude in his eyes. "I can't bring myself to think about what … what … if Joy hadn't saved you! What might have happened."

"But Joy *did* save me, and all is well."

Aaron nodded. "Thank you so much, Joy."

"As I said to your aunt, I would do it again. You are such a sweet and kind young man, Aaron. There is hope for the future of the planet, with young people such as yourself." I turned to Ariadne. "Aaron mentioned that you're taking him around the world when he gets his AA degree."

"True! I'm already looking forward to it."

"Me too!" Aaron brightened considerably.

"That's quite the graduation present. I imagine you'll get as much education from that experience as you'll have gotten from the two years of college."

"I believe it will be more," Aaron said quietly.

Ariadne chuckled. "He's not overly fond of formal education."

"It has its pluses, and it has its minuses," I suggested. "Keep in mind that the pluses have as much to do with the professional peers you'll meet in the course of education as it has to do with your classes. One of my best friends is

Professor Carlton Mayes, who helped me sort out what happened to your aunt. A formal education is more than merely what you learn in classrooms."

"Good point," Aaron said. "I shall keep it in mind when I'm yawning in class."

Ariadne looked at him affectionately. "I'll box your ears, young man!"

"Please do," he leaned toward her.

She tousled his hair instead. "Love you!"

"Love you more," Aaron returned.

Teaspoon *yip, yip, yipped*, jumping back and forth from one lap to the other.

I felt just a bit uncomfortable and intrusive in the intimate family moment.

Ariadne glanced up at me. "I'm glad you're here to witness firsthand what a wonderful thing you've done for our family by saving me."

I nodded shyly.

"Joy and I have just been talking about how Detective Rusch figured out how Lowell stole '*Blue Trees,*'" she said to Aaron.

"*What a sick creep!*" Aaron blurted. "Makes my skin crawl to think about him skulking through Aunt Ariadne's house."

"Yes, a disconcertingly sick individual. But let's not give him any more of our precious energy. I've been thinking about the next theme for my Wall of Art. I've loved the *Blue Wall,* but it's time to put this awful experience behind us, and changing out the art is a way to move forward."

"That's an excellent idea," I agreed. "I'll be most curious to hear about it."

"Hear about it? Goodness, I hope you accept my invitation to the little party I always have when I change out the art."

"Oh!" I gasped. "I accept right now! That means a lot to me, thank you. I can't wait to see what the next theme is!"

As we sat there for a few moments in quiet reverie, I heard a bevy of melodic voices seeming to approach nearby.

Chapter 21

Five Ladybirds A-Singing

A nd in fact, yes! The *Ladybirds* in all their pastel, flowing splendor, along with Possum wearing a red filmy blouse with black polka dots and a red skirt, looking so much like a ladybug herself, came out onto the patio via the driveway, their little Yorkies leading the way.

Aaron jumped up and gathered chairs in a circle. Sophia, Elgin, Elvira, Mary, and Possum sat, all chatting at once, while Teaspoon jumped down from Ariadne's lap to greet her canine friends.

"Oh, Ariadne, I'm so relieved you're all right!" Sophia breathed, reaching across the circle to give her hands a squeeze.

"Yes, yes, so relieved, so happy!" all the *Ladybirds* and Possum cooed.

"Thank you my dears! I felt your love while captive. It was stressful, but I had the strongest feeling that help would be coming. I worried, of course, about poor little Teaspoon, who I believed was miserable. But then I learned that she was at Joy's house, being indulged and entertained by a bio cat and a robo cat, and probably didn't miss me in the least!"

Teaspoon jumped back onto Ariadne's lap at the mention of her name.

"Oh no," I protested. "She missed you. It was a relief that Robbie was so attentive to her, and they played wonderfully. But several times I heard Teaspoon whimpering, and I knew the only thing I could do to make her happy would be to find you!"

Teaspoon jumped across to my lap, looking up at me, like "where *is* Robbie, anyway?" I laughed. "She heard me say 'R-o-b-b-i-e.' Well, your mom says you can have a play date, so you'll get to see him one day soon."

"*Yip-yip!*" Teaspoon declared. She jumped down again to play with the little Yorkies, who had been let off their tangled leashes, performing antics that had us all giggling.

"Dear Ariadne," Elgin said, "we have a little surprise for you. Actually, it's sort of a surprise for us as well. We just discovered, the day that Joy saved you, that our own Possum has a beautiful singing voice. But not only that! She has surprised us with a stunning ability to write music and lyrics. And so in honor of our delight and relief to have you back safely in our midst, we have this musical offering for you."

The four *Ladybirds* stood up, and Mary sounded a note on a pitch pipe. They softly hummed a beautiful four-part melody, and then broke into a chorus:

> *Alive and well, alive and well!*
> *In the soul of love we dwell!*

They softly sang, so beautifully, a cappella. I noticed Possum holding her head down, overcome with shyness.

They sang the chorus again, and finally, Elgin stepped forward and made Possum stand up. Elgin stepped back in line, and, reluctantly, Possum stood in her little Ladybird outfit, in front of the towering, pastel beauties.

Softly she began to sing the verse, while the four *Ladybirds* hummed accompaniment in the background.

> *"We are filled with delight*
> *That you're alive and well!*
> *Our hearts' candles alight,*
> *In the soul of love we dwell!"*

She began. I could barely hear her, the *Ladybirds* sang yet more softly. Then Possum closed her eyes, and let herself fall into the music. Her voice rose above the *Ladybirds*, it swelled and rose above the patio, above the trees and up into the sky, where the ladybugs were known to fly.

Her voice was breath-taking, almost mystical, beautiful beyond belief. It far surpassed the little snippet we'd heard downstairs from her apartment. She continued to sing the song of her own creation, sharing the love she had for every person and every creature in Ariadne's backyard.

> *Alive and well, alive and well,*
> *In the soul of love we dwell!*
>
> *May you be joyful in the day*
> *At night may peace prevail*
> *This is what we pray*
> *May we all be alive and well!*
>
> *Alive and well, alive and well,*
> *In the soul of love we dwell!*

She sang, and as the song came to a close, her voice softened, while the *Ladybirds* took up the chorus;

> *Alive and well, alive and well,*
> *In the soul of love we dwell,*
> *In the soul of love we dwell!*

When the song ended, Ariadne, Aaron, and I sat for a few moments, stupefied. It was more than we could possibly have anticipated. But, finally, I began to clap wildly, joined by Aaron and Ariadne, and someone behind me! I turned to see Travis at the side of the patio, as transfixed by the talent as I was.

"That was beyond amazing, thank you so much," Ariadne said. "This is certainly the silver lining to my having been kidnapped, if it inspires such wondrous talent!"

Travis grabbed a chair and sat by me. "Incredible!" he leaned over and whispered. "What talent!"

"Detective Rusch!" Ariadne came to him and shook his hand. "Thank you for coming to my little Welcome Home party. I'm so glad you could make it."

"Thank you for inviting me. Little did I know I would be treated to such remarkable talent!"

"Nor I! My goodness, Possum, you have really been hiding your light under a bushel. But that's over now. You must share you gift with others. It's extremely inspiring."

Possum ducked her head, looking as if she wished she could turn into a real [, and crawl away across the lawn. "Thank you. You are being very kind, I'm sure," she said.

"Do you really not know how beautiful your voice is?" I asked, incredulous.

"No. I don't, actually. I mean, I have to take your word for it. I know it feels good when I sing, but I'm not sure how it sounds."

"Well," Travis said, nodding emphatically, "it's beautiful! I don't know when I've been so moved by a live performance. You all are going to make me want to go to church!"

The women giggled, and I, for one, thought it not a bad idea for him to go to that inspiring service.

The *Ladybirds* returned to their seats. "We are now a quintet!" Sophia proclaimed, looking as proud as if she'd discovered Possum's talent by herself.

"Lovely!" Ariadne said. "I'm with Travis, I'm going to have to finagle my schedule around to be sure to get to your performances. Please let me know when you're scheduled!"

"Will do," Mary said, making a note on her wrist comp.

The women all began chatting, discussing their favorite songs and what all. I wasn't really paying attention. I was distracted by Travis sitting by me. I looked over at him, and he caught my eye. "Can we talk later about the reward money, Joy?" he said softly. "I need to know your banking info, or where you want me to deposit it. This isn't the most graceful moment to approach it, but my boss wants it cleared up."

"Oh! Well, why are you asking me? It's not mine."

"Ahm, it most certainly is."

Ariadne overheard Travis. "Indeed it is your money, Joy, with profound gratitude from me and my family, for whom it's a mere drop in a bucket."

Everyone became quiet.

"Well, my buckets are of a considerably different size, but I really do not need that sort of money. I'll take the fee I would charge for the time invested in the, shall I say, 'project.' But more than that … I would not be comfortable taking. Please, Ariadne, after I invoice the amount, please put the balance in your favorite project."

"I will put it, if you insist, in the project *you* find most meaningful. Otherwise, I will not accept the money. And you'll get Travis in trouble with his boss." She grinned mischievously.

"Okay, that sounds like something I'd enjoy. I'll sit down with you sometime soon and determine my favorite cause."

"Excellent!" Ariadne declared.

The women returned to their banter, with a promise of a second song from the *five* lovely *Ladybirds*.

A perfectly divine evening!

I peeked over at Travis, so relaxed and enjoying himself. Looking great in street clothes. He felt my glance and turned to contemplate me.

Oh, those incredible hazel eyes! They took my breath away. I screwed up my courage and asked, "What about that dinner invitation?"

Don't miss the next book in the *Joy Forest Mystery Series*!
Check it out at: *https://shop.blytheayne.com*.
Here's the first two chapters of *A Haras of Horses....*

A Haras of Horses

Blythe Ayne

Chapter 1

A Horse Named Grifter

Aunt Claudia's jangling phone ring tore me from my
concentration.

The disruption meant that, *whatever* my aunt had to
say, I'd have to drop everything. But for a few moments, I
willfully continued building the 3-D nuralnet of my Kashmir project.

The jangling abused my nerves again. I sighed. "Hold," I
commanded the nuralnet. The beautiful translucent colors of

the 3-D that surrounded me shrank to a bubble hovering over my desk. I swiveled my chair around, turning my back on my work.

"Hi, Aunt Claudia. What's up?" Yes, I would rather have said, "Dear Aunt Claudia, could you please call me in the evening, instead of interrupting my work day?" But I restrained myself.

"What's up is that horse of yours," she said without greeting or preamble.

"Grifter?"

"Do you have another horse?"

"No, Aunt Claudia. Grifter is my only much-adored-but-expensive horse. What's going on with Grifter?" I rarely had time to be with Grifter, but I loved him with all my heart, and I didn't want any bad news.

"Well, the bad news is …."

Dang! I just told fate to not give me any bad news.

Aunt Claudia rattled on, "he's whining. Whining and whining. It's driving me nuts."

"Whining? Do you mean 'whinnying'?"

"No, Joy. I do not mean whinnying. I know what I'm saying, please do not patronize me."

"No. No patronizing, Aunt Claudia. It's just, you know, people don't usually refer to any sound that a horse makes as 'whining.'"

"He's whining," Aunt Claudia insisted. "He sounds like a … I don't know … he sounds like a child, or a dog. *Whine! Whine! Whine!* That's all he does."

I stood up and paced up and back, up and back. Robbie the robo cat joined me, pacing up and back alongside me. I couldn't quite imagine Grifter whining. He was not a brave horse, but he rarely complained about anything. "Is he eating?"

"Yes," at Claudia said. Then she giggled, a sound I rarely heard from her. "He's eating like a horse."

"Oh, yeah, eating like a horse, ha ha, funny. So, that's good. Is he whining right now?"

"Probably."

"You can't hear him?"

"He's out in the pasture, along the fence, his head hanging over into the neighbors field."

I wondered how that was relevant, but I was so concerned about Grifter "whining"—whatever that meant—that I didn't go into it. "Is he not well?"

"There doesn't seem to be anything wrong with him," Aunt Claudia said, becoming yet more testy.

"What does Uncle Eben say about Grifter whining?"

"Well, I don't know."

"You haven't asked him?" This seemed improbable, as Aunt Claudia was *always* bending Uncle Eben's ear with one complaint or another.

"No I didn't ask him. I've been *telling* him. Grifter's whining is making me lose my mind."

"Is Uncle Eben there?"

"He's in town, getting groceries." I could just sense Aunt Claudia tapping her foot with my, I'm sure she thought, extreme obtuseness.

I looked over my shoulder at the little 3-D bubble of my project hovering over the desk, and felt it receding from getting done by its deadline. "Has the vet looked at Grifter?"

"Yes, your uncle had Charley come out. They stood in the pasture with Grifter and shot the breeze for *two hours*. When they came back in, Charley said there wasn't anything physically wrong with the horse. He said he thought Grifter was lonely. Since we got rid of the three sheep, he's the only creature on the property, except for the field mice and raccoons."

"If he's just lonely, the only thing I could do is buy another horse to keep him company," I said. Dollar signs floated away in front of my mind's eye.

"Oh heavens, Joy, *do not* get another horse! One is too many."

I refused to agree with her, although she was frustratingly correct.

"I can't come right now. I'm in the middle of a huge...."

"I know, Joy, you're in the middle of a huge project. You're always in the middle of a huge project. But really, if you don't do something about this horse noise, I guess I'll have to."

Was she threatening me? I could feel my brow furrow. "What does that mean?"

"I might have to put him up for sale."

Now I was getting angry. One of my life lessons was to learn how to not let Aunt Claudia get under my skin, like she was doing now. "No, you won't, Aunt Claudia," I said with quiet reserve. "He's my horse, I have the papers to prove it, and you will not sell my horse. Anyway, Uncle Eben wouldn't let you."

Although I was pushing her about as far as I've ever pushed, I knew I had her there. Uncle Eben would never allow Grifter to be sold out from under me, even setting aside the fact that his ownership papers were in my name and in my safe. *So, take that, dear Auntie!*

I sighed in resignation. "I'll come out tomorrow morning, Aunt Claudia. But if I'm going to do that I've really got to get to work right now. I'll see you in the morning. Much love to you and Uncle Eben. Bye now." I hung up without waiting for a response.

* *

"**P**leeeaze let me come with you, Joy. I want to meet Grifter," Robbie nagged me the next morning, standing on his hind legs, his front paws together prayerfully.

"No, Robbie," I said, tearing around my bedroom, trying to think of everything I needed, knowing full well I would leave the most important something behind.

"But …."

"Robbie, please. I must think." I stood looking into my backpack, trying to imagine what I was forgetting.

"AR glasses," Robbie said.

"Right." I grabbed them up and put them in the backpack. I threw my hands up. "That'll have to do. I've gotta get on the road."

I picked up the backpack and turned. *Arg!* Robbie's expression was hard to ignore. "Don't try to work me Robbie, dear. If it was just you, it wouldn't be much of a problem. But packing up Dickens, and worrying about him there …."

"I'll take care of him!"

"Yes, you will. Right here, thank you kindly. I'll take you to meet Grifter some other time, when … when …."

"When Grifter isn't whining?"

"Yes. When Grifter isn't whining." I reached over to pet Dickens, in his usual spot, curled up asleep on the bed, then stooped over to pet Robbie. "I'm counting on you, you know. I'm running off half-cocked, and I need you to be my eyes and ears here at the home front. Okay, I *must go.*"

Robbie followed me to the back door, while I ordered my car to come into the drive, but he stopped begging me to come along, which was a relief.

"Okay my furry friend, I'm off."

"When will you be back?"

"*Oh!*" The thought had not yet crossed my mind. "I … I don't know. In a couple days, I hope. You'll be the first to know, Robbie." I stepped out the back door, threw my backpack into the backseat of the car and climbed in. "Uncle Eben's," I ordered.

"Oh! Road trip!" The car exclaimed. "It's been a while."

"Yes, it's been a while." I didn't feel like idle chat at the moment. I needed to dictate into my wrist comp a few points I must not forget about to my disrupted Kashmir project. And then I needed to get ready to be with Aunt Claudia—not the easiest experience. But most importantly, I needed to think about Grifter. What could possibly be wrong with him?

It was only a two hour drive to my childhood home outside of Leavenworth Washington, not nearly enough time to do all the thinking I needed to think.

Suddenly, Aunt Claudia's raucous phone ring jolted me out of my dark reverie.

Chapter 2
The Old Home Place

I pulled into the driveway. "What's up Aunt Claudia?"

"Where *are* you?" she squawked.

"In the driveway! What's the urgency?"

Without answering, she hung up.

I got out of the car and reached in the back for my backpack. As I did so I heard a horrible sound like some machinery was about to quit working. I stepped inside the little mid-twentieth century farmhouse, ready to give my aunt and uncle their hugs. But I could see Aunt Claudia was not in a hug-receiving mood, her body tense, her brow furrowed. Uncle Eben was nowhere to be seen.

"Where's Uncle Eben?"

"In the pasture, with your horse."

"Oh dear! Is he really sick?"

"Why would you ask that?" She asked in a testy voice. "There's nothing wrong with your uncle."

"Goodness! I'm not asking if Uncle Eben is sick! I'm asking if Grifter is sick."

Things have reached a new level of wacky around here, I thought.

"Well, Joy, we just don't know. Now that you're here, he had better calm down. And I mean your horse, not your uncle!"

I guffawed out loud. "Oh, Aunt Claudia, you made a joke!" I went up to her and forced a hug upon her whether she liked it or not. That weird machine sound seemed to augment as we stood there in the awkward hug my aunt refused to return.

"What is this weird sound, Aunt Claudia? It's like some machinery is falling apart."

"That weird sound, Morning Joy, is your horse!"

Wow! We were in unchartered territory for my aunt to call me by my birth name, which was rarely mentioned. "That sound is Grifter?! How is it *possible*?"

I didn't even bother to go to my tiny childhood bedroom to throw down my backpack. I flung it on the sofa on the way out the back door. "We'll get to the bottom of this, Auntie, don't worry," I said, worrying enough for both of us. I'd never heard such a sound from any creature in my life!

Grifter was out in the pasture, head hanging over the fence, making the huge and piteous sound. I hurried up to him and Uncle Eben, who was patting him, and making soothing sounds, that had no effect on Grifter, whatsoever.

Uncle Eben was on the far side of Grifter and didn't see me approach. "Hello Uncle Eben, what's going on with Grifter?" I said in the lull between two bouts of Grifter's weird noise.

"*Oh! Joy!* You startled me," he said, peering around Grifter's neck. "We have no idea what's wrong with him. He makes this, how would you describe it? *sound*, pretty much all day, and into the night. Sometimes even in his sleep! The vet said it was the weirdest thing he'd ever encountered."

"Yeah. Weird." I tried to pull Grifter's head from hanging over the fence, but he wouldn't let me. It cut me to the quick that he didn't even acknowledge me. "But Uncle Eben, there's something seriously wrong with him! How is it possible Charley didn't find anything?"

"I don't know, Joy. I really don't know. I agree with you, but if the doctor can't find anything, what are we to do?"

This was a new sort of mystery. I stood there petting my sad, depressed horse, contemplating what might cause him to make this noise. One of the many things I loved about Grifter, even though he's not the most beautiful horse in the world, is that he's *different*, different in a lot of sweet and wonderful ways. Always, until this moment, attentive to me, able to practically read my mind. Or, more accurately, my heart.

Being raised by Aunt Claudia had not been the easiest. But Grifter, in my life since I was twelve, always soothed the pain. Yes, Uncle Eben was there. After any of Aunt Claudia's many tirades, later, out in the barn, he'd give me affection and support. But he still always defended Aunt Claudia's indefensible position.

Only Grifter understood the way my heart hurt. And now I saw it was *my* turn to take care of *him*. This terrible sound was grief, and if my presence didn't calm him, something other than my absence was the cause.

Like I say, a new mystery.

"I could hear him crying from the driveway, Uncle Eben! I thought a piece of machinery was breaking down. I can see why Aunt Claudia is at her wit's end." I had to practically shout to be heard above Grifter.

Uncle Eben came around Grifter and stood beside me. "Let's go to the barn," he said, "where can hear ourselves."

I nodded, reluctant to leave Grifter now that I was here. We walked uphill to the cool, shadowy barn, and found a couple of bales of straw to sit on.

"What's going on, Uncle Eben? If Charley is convinced that Grifter is not dealing with some physical malady, yet he's showing such profound distress, and *more to the point*, not even acknowledging me, there is something causing his grief."

Uncle Eben picked up a stick and poked it around in the straw at his feet. We both studied his moves as if the answers to our questions would magically appear in the straw like tea leaves in the bottom of a cup. "I think you're right, Joy." He paused. "I think you're right. Though it seems too huge a reaction for…."

I held my breath waiting for him to tell me what Grifter's huge reaction might be attributed to. Finally, losing my patience, I asked, "For what, Uncle Eben, for *what?*"

"Well, Grifter had established a bond with a horse that lived next door. I'd noticed that he spent all of his time when not in the barn where he is right now. Head over the fence looking into the neighbor's pasture." Uncle Eben glanced up at me and then back down at his handiwork stirring up the straw. It seemed he felt guilty. Strange. I kept my silence.

"I hate to admit this, but I really didn't pay much attention to Grifter. He appeared content. But when that horse next-door disappeared I…."

"*Disappeared!* What do you mean, the horse next door disappeared?"

"Just that. The guy next door bought that gorgeous black Arabian stud, did you happen to see him?"

I nodded. I'd noticed the beautiful horse, but I didn't know that Grifter was attached to him.

Uncle Eben continued. "Strangely enough, that black stallion befriended Grifter. Particularly strange, given that he had three beautiful mares to keep him occupied. Anyway, one day that black horse was gone. Then I heard through the rumor mill that he'd been stolen."

I sighed as I saw my near future changing, shifting away from getting back to my present home and my present obligations. "Criminitly Uncle Eben, that's terrible! What does the neighbor say?" I'd never met the current neighbors, who'd moved in only a couple years ago.

"Well, Joy I know this probably seems a little weird but I've never talked to him. Ahm … that's not quite accurate. I tried a couple times. But if you think your Aunt Claudia is difficult, she is a Sunday school picnic in comparison to that guy."

This was shocking. Everyone adores my Uncle Eben, the sweetest, most easy-going person on the planet. And he never said anything bad about anyone, no matter how much they'd earned it. I particularly noted his negative comment about the neighbor.

"Are you sure he didn't just sell the horse, or move him somewhere else?" I asked.

"No. I've heard it from Charley, and from Myles, both reputable enough, and I've heard it elsewhere as well. It's kind of a big deal, because I guess that stud is famous in horse circles. And you know, we have our horse circles here."

Oh yes I knew, it was a horsey community.

But … a horse thief. Very serious business.

Just then, I heard Grifter screaming. I jumped up and ran out into the pasture.

About the Author:

Thank you for reading *A Gaggle of Geese*. Be sure to read all of Joy Forest's mysterious adventures, which take place in the world of the near future.

Here's a bit about me, if you're curious. I live near where Joy lives, but I'm in the present, about ten years before where Joy's story begins. Unless you're reading this ten years from now, and then, well, I'm in the past, and you're in Joy's present.

I live in the midst (and often the mist) of ten acres of forest, with domestic and wild creatures as family and companions. Here I create an ever-growing inventory of fiction and nonfiction books, short stories, illustrated kid's books, vast amounts of poetry, and the occasional article. I've also begun audio recording my books, which, having a background in performance, I find quite enjoyable.

I throw a bit of wood carving in when I need a change of pace. And I'm frequently on a ladder, cleaning my gutters. There's something spectacular about being on a ladder—the vista opens up all around, and one feels rather like a bird or a squirrel, perched on a metal branch.

After I received my Doctorate from the University of California at Irvine in the School of Social Sciences, (majoring in psychology and ethnography—surprisingly similar to Joy's scholarly background), I moved to the Pacific Northwest to write and to have a modest private psychotherapy practice in a small town not much bigger than a village.

Finally, I decided it was time to put my full focus on my writing, where, through the world-shrinking internet, I could "meet" greater numbers of people. *Where I could meet you!*

All the creatures in my forest and I are glad you "stopped by." Thank you so much for any reviews or comments you may share. We writers create in a void, and hearing from *YOU* makes all the difference.

Blythe@BlytheAyne.com

And here's my website, and my *Boutique of Books*:

www.BlytheAyne.com

https://shop.BlytheAyne.com

'Til We Meet Again,
Blythe

Made in United States
North Haven, CT
06 May 2023

36184484R10114